THE WORLD OF
SUPERSAURS
THE STEGOSORCERER

JAY JAY BURRIDGE

First published in Great Britain in 2018 by
Supersaurs
80-81 Wimpole Street, London, W1G 9RE
www.supersaurs.com

Text and illustrations copyright © Supersaurs Limited, 2018
Illustrations by Chris West & Jay Jay Burridge

A CIP catalogue record for this book is available from the British Library.

ISBN: 978-1- 786-96802-9

1 2 3 4 5 6 7 8 9 10

Typeset in Adobe Jenson by Perfect Bound Ltd
Printed and bound by Toppan Leefung

Supersaurs is an imprint of Bonnier Zaffre,
a Bonnier Publishing Company

www.bonnierpublishing.co.uk

For Mouse, Bear and Fox
and all the other creatures in my life.

ASIA

PACIFIC

NORTHERN
INDIAN OCEAN
OCEAN

SOUTHERN

INDIAN OCEAN

SAURIA TRADING
COMPANY

OCEAN

Arrival by Boat

~ the ship's pet ~

Port of Mombasa, Kenya, 1932

Carter Kingsley woke with a start in a tangle of black feathers. The *Orca* was anchored where the harbourmaster had instructed, safely offshore. There was a thud to the ship's hull. He sat up, blinked the sleep from his eyes, and rubbed his nose. The tyrant slept on beside him, its sides moving rhythmically as it breathed. Dawn was breaking in streaks of deep orange over the small steamer boat, which listed at an angle.

'Carter, you awake?'

The call came from the wheelhouse, where Captain Wilbur Woods was extinguishing his lantern.

'Captain, yes!' Carter leapt to his feet.

'We have important company – behave yourself,' the captain told him.

Carter looked quizzically at the captain. Spoken words were still confusing for him when joined up in long sentences, and in conversation Carter relied on gestures and emotions to understand what was being said. The captain pointed to where three men dressed in smart uniforms had made their way aboard from their smaller launch, which continued to thud rhythmically against the *Orca*'s hull. He gave Carter a warning look to let him know the situation was serious.

The captain slid down the broken steps to the deck. The three men stood for a moment and looked towards Carter, before the tallest of them saluted and handed a bundle of papers over to the captain. Carter saluted back, but was ignored.

'Good morning, Captain Woods. Your passengers' papers all check out. However we still have an issue with your cargo.'

The man unbuttoned the chest pocket of his jacket and took out a small, well-worn book. Dramatically, he flicked through all the pages, from beginning to end, then slammed it shut.

'This book is the law. It informs me of the class and value applied to everything that may pass through the Port of Mombasa. My job as head of customs is to ensure that the law is strictly adhered to.'

Captain Woods nodded. 'I have docked here many times before, sir.'

'That may be so,' the head of customs replied, 'but this is the first time you have imported a wild saur, Captain Woods, and, more to the point, one that my book – the law – does not list: a Black Flores Tyrant.'

'A Black Dwarf Tyrant, from Flores,' the captain corrected him, and shrugged. 'First time for everything?'

'Indeed. It is also the first time I have seen a saur of this kind uncaged or unshackled. There are laws regarding this as well, and that is why the harbourmaster won't allow your vessel to dock. How many shiphands did you start your voyage with?' The head of customs pointed towards Carter, who nervously stepped back into the warmth of the sleeping tyrant. 'Is he the last one left?'

The two men standing beside him started to chuckle, then realised the head of customs wasn't making a joke.

'This is Carter Kingsley, and this is his tyrant,' said the captain.

The head of customs looked at the boy with scorn, before replying, 'Tyrants are reserved for kings and emperors, or the immortal gods; not scruffy children, Captain Woods.'

Captain Woods looked to Carter, then said: 'Your book, sir, the law – it mentions importing wild saurs, and the rules thereof?'

'Correct.'

'Well, this is not a wild saur,' the captain replied. 'It belongs to Carter. It's the ship's pet.'

'The ship's pet?'

The men sniggered again, and this time the head of customs joined in.

'Pets roll around and fetch sticks. This is a wild tyrant, unlisted in my law book, and thus not permitted to pass through the Port of Mombasa.'

Carter watched the conversation between the men, trying to decipher what it was about. Laughter usually meant everyone was happy, but the captain was not laughing, so something was not right. As the men's laughter grew in volume, the tyrant opened its eyes and lifted its head.

The men instantly stopped laughing.

Carter patted the tyrant's nose and smoothed out some of its crumpled feathers on the side the saur had been lying on.

Captain Woods picked up a chewed length of wood the size of a fence post, and handed it to Carter.

'Trick,' he mouthed.

Carter understood what had to be done. He looked at the men, who had all retreated as far from the tyrant as the ship's deck would let them, turned to the tyrant and whistled. The reaction was instant. The tyrant scrambled to its feet and revealed its huge bulk, bobbed its head, opened its mouth wide and drooled.

'Hold onto something,' Captain Woods told the men, gesturing at the rail of the ship, as he wound his own hand around some rope hanging from the mast.

Carter swung the wooden stake around his head twice, before hurling it as far as he could. They all watched it splash into the sea.

The tyrant stared intently as the stake popped up to the surface. Carter let out another shrill whistle. Like a coiled spring, the tyrant leapt from the deck into the sea, sending the ship into a violent rocking motion that knocked the customs officers to the floor.

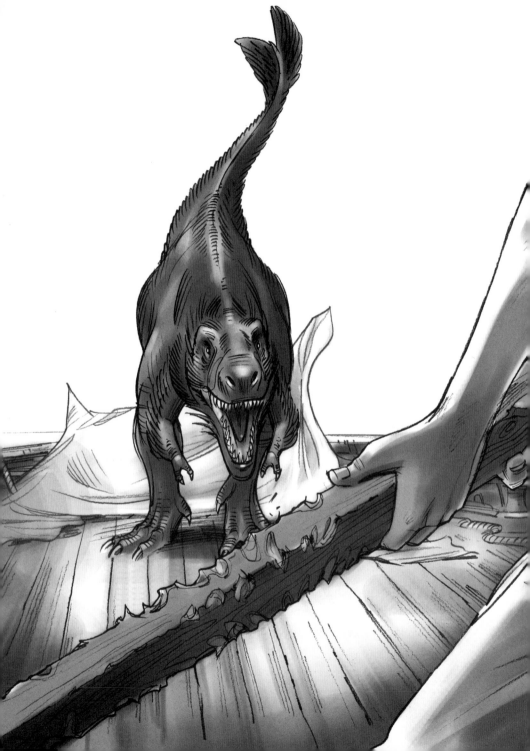

By the time the *Orca* had righted itself and the men had got to their feet, the tyrant was already swimming back with the length of wood in its mouth, like a dog retrieving a stick from a pond. Carter leant over the side, and tugged at the wooden stake gripped firmly in its sharp teeth.

'Drop.'

The tyrant let go, sending Carter stumbling backwards. The customs officers were open-mouthed in shock.

Carter patted the tyrant's nose, then said: 'Fish!'

The tyrant ducked under the water, and resurfaced on the other side of the ship.

'What's it doing now?' asked the bewildered head of customs.

'Catching breakfast,' Captain Woods replied. 'You'd better hold on this time; getting it back on board is a bit tricky.'

The men gripped the rail tightly, their eyes wide in astonishment as they watched the tyrant swim and duck under the ship's hull once more. The water was still.

Captain Woods went to a large winch at the stern, and took the handle in his hands. Carter stood motionless, one arm held high, until the tyrant resurfaced behind the boat with something large in its mouth. Carter dropped his arm and the captain wound the winch. A submerged platform rose up through the water at the stern.

The tyrant swam to the platform, its catch still held in its mouth, and climbed on. The customs men, eyes agog, clung to the rail and looked on in astonishment as the tyrant was hauled upwards out of the sea. It came back on board with a wet thud. Eager to please, the tyrant dipped its head, came in close to the officers and dropped the back half of a large fish at their feet. All three men did their best to back away from it, but were trapped by the ship's rail.

Then the tyrant stepped back and shook itself down. Starting at its head, waves of spray lifted off its sleek body down to its tail and then back up again, sending arcs of fine seawater everywhere. The three customs officers caught the full force of the spray, and were soaked to the skin.

Puffed back up to its original size, the tyrant looked at Carter, who said 'Sit', and it plopped itself down on the spot.

Captain Woods smiled at Carter, and gave him a thumbs up.

'As I told you,' the captain said, addressing the dripping wet men, 'this is no wild tyrant.' He gestured as he spoke the next question, so Carter would understand him. 'Carter, what's your tyrant's name?'

'Buster,' said Carter. 'He Buster.'

'There,' the captain said. 'His pet's called Buster. I trust everything's now in order for us to go ashore?'

2

Welcome to the Human Race

~ every scar and bump ~

The harbourmaster, and everyone at the port who had ears, had heard of the tyrant's tricks well before Captain Wilbur Woods moored the *Orca* between two large cargo ships at the dock. Carter had fashioned a rope around the tyrant's neck so it could safely be led off the boat. After all, the captain had explained, the loophole in the law had to be seen to be taken seriously. Carter knew that Buster, despite his antics as an eager pet on board, was not really reliable around strange noises, people or other animals, of which there were many gathered on the dockside. A crowd watched in awe as Carter led the huge creature ashore. The mass of onlookers parted to let Carter lead the tyrant over to a water butt, where it lapped away at the fresh water, its tail wagging happily as it quenched its thirst, sending the crowd hastily scattering in order not to be knocked flying. Beatrice Kingsley ran up to her

little brother and hugged him tightly, her face shining with pride.

'Carter, you did it! Well done. We heard that the customs officers were stunned into letting you dock.'

'Terrified, more like!' joined in Theodore Logan, grinning as he arrived beside them.

Carter shrugged and smiled happily.

Theodore left them with the tyrant and boarded the *Orca*, where he gave Captain Woods an apologetic shrug.

'Sorry, Wilbur,' he said. 'They wouldn't take my word for it that the tyrant was safe.'

'Would *you* have?' the captain replied.

'No,' admitted Theodore. He nodded at the dockside. 'Looks like her ladyship's here.'

Barbara Brownlee twirled her umbrella elegantly, half to give an air of elegance to the dirty dockside and half to ward people out of her way. As Theodore steadied the gangway for her, Bea looked over at her grandmother with a smile. Her opinion of Bunty had changed drastically since their time on Aru. Before, the sight of Theodore helping Bunty get on and off things, especially boats, had been something Bea had rolled her eyes at in frustration; now the familiar sight made her feel gratitude towards the woman who dominated both her and Theodore's lives. Her godfather must have picked up on Bea's thoughts as he looked up for a moment and gave Bea one of his charismatic winks. She smiled back. Theodore was grateful to be in the position to help Bunty, even though he knew her well enough to guess that some sort of pointed comment was about to be bestowed on them.

Sure enough, Bunty was right on cue. She gave Carter a sharp look, along with a sniff of disapproval.

'He needs a haircut,' she announced. 'Can you take care of it, Theodore? There's a barber on the quayside.'

Theodore looked at Carter's long, thick, matted hair.

'That's going to be a challenge,' he muttered. Her instructions given, Bunty took Theodore's hand and allowed him to help her on board, where she began organising.

'I've made arrangements for someone to look over the *Orca*, Captain Woods,' Bunty announced.

The makeshift alterations to the stern, the many broken floorboards, smashed handrails, cracked windows and scratched paintwork were the price of a long voyage with the tyrant. The once glorious ship needed proper attention and, as promised, Bunty was to foot the bill.

'The bilge pump has been working at full pelt for weeks now, and I fear the incident with the lipleurodon may have cracked the hull,' said the captain. 'But don't worry, the boatyards around Mombasa Docks have got everything needed to bring the *Orca* back to tip-top condition.'

Bunty passed him a fat envelope. 'Here are the contact details of my safari lodge, and some money to cover things in my absence,' she told him. 'Do let us know when everything on the *Orca* is ready for our final leg back to England.'

Captain Woods looked to his listing boat, which seemed to not only bob higher up out of the water without the unsettling weight of the tyrant but also to slip perilously closer to the waterline.

'I may need some time.' He wiped his brow with his soft cap.

'Good,' Bunty chirped. 'So do we. We have a long journey to the lodge anyway, and I would like to spend some time there.'

Theodore picked up the bags that had been waiting for them on the deck. Unlike previous journeys, because of what had happened to them on Aru, the amount of luggage this time was small.

'Looks like this is goodbye for the moment, my friend,' he said to the captain. 'Until the next time we meet, take good care of yourself.'

✦ ✦ ✦

Carter sat in the barber's chair as it was pumped upwards, and as his reflection appeared in the mirror in front of him, he stared, and then turned and smiled at Theodore in delight. Seeing his reflection like this, so large, was a first.

The barber, however, was not smiling. He surveyed Carter's long matted locks doubtfully, wondering where to begin, and looked helplessly at Theodore.

Theodore shrugged, feeling just as helpless, but he was also concerned about what Bunty's reaction would be if he failed to get Carter's hair fit for polite society.

'Do what you can,' he said.

The barber took a comb and started teasing Carter's matted locks apart, but immediately the comb jammed. After a few unsuccessful attempts to get the comb out, the barber tried cutting it free, but the first pair of scissors had no impact on Carter's hair, and the second pair broke in half.

He looked at Theodore again and shook his head.

'There's only one way to do this,' he said, 'and that's to take it all off.'

'All off?' echoed Theodore, worried what Bunty would say when she saw a shaven-headed Carter.

'It's not just the hair, it's the lice,' the barber told him.

Theodore sighed.

'Carter,' he said sombrely, 'this is going to be a big change.'

Carter looked at him, puzzled. Then he saw the barber produce a very large pair of shears.

Alarmed, he began to climb out of the chair, but Theodore put a gentle, restraining hand on the boy's shoulder. 'Trust me,' he said. 'It'll be all right, I promise.'

Carter hesitated, watching Theodore's face in the mirror, then reluctantly retook his position in the chair.

Theodore nodded. 'Good boy.'

As the barber set to work, Carter sat upright, his eyes fixed on his reflection in the mirror.

It was a long and hard job, but finally Carter's locks were strewn on the floor. His shaven head showed every scar and bump, each one a poignant reminder of being raised by raptors in the jungles of Aru.

From behind his chair, Theodore looked into the mirror at Carter. Carter caught Theodore's glance, and a smile spread across his lips.

'Welcome to the human race,' said Theodore.

3

Something Strange

~ an accident waiting to happen ~

On the dockside, Theodore slung a line of rope over Buster's back to attach Grace and Franklin's old trunk, Theodore's kit bag and Bea's small case to the tyrant, as Bunty waited in the shade. Carter looked on in awe as a whole steam locomotive was unloaded by a huge crane, then gently manoeuvred by two large brachios. Beside him, Bea studied her brother's new haircut. Or, rather, what was left of his hair after the barber had gone to work. Which, it had to be admitted, was very little. In fact, none. Now there was just … well … a shaved head, pitted with ancient scars.

Carter didn't seem to care, though. All his attention was on the brachios, an expression of wonder on his face as he watched the huge creatures deal with the train. A few shorthorn tritops and a third brachio were handling wooden cases alongside them. These brachios were a lot bigger than the ones Carter had first seen in India a few weeks earlier. There they had been decorated with colourful reins and body paint; here they were bound by chains and rope.

Carter was a fast learner and had already mastered some words, as well as human body language, which most people took for granted. Bea knew the steam locomotive would be hard to explain, but they were heading to the railway station later, where Carter would find it easier to understand. She'd opted to point out to Carter how the men saddled to the brachios' necks – the drivers –were controlling them by sending various commands up long bamboo poles that spurred out from either side of their shoulders. These supported lines of thin cord that led to the brachios' head braces, to which differently pitched bells were attached.

'Up, down, left, right, stop, slow; every command has a different bell,' said Bea. 'Ding-a-ling.' She rang a small imaginary bell next to her left ear before swinging around to the left. She then repeated it again by her right ear and swung over to the right.

Carter nodded and rung his own imaginary bell above his head before looking up, then did the same below and looked down. 'Ding-a-ling' and a few gestures had explained it all.

Bea knew that they were being watched. It was understandable that the people in Mombasa regarded them with curiosity. However she was blissfully unaware there was a pair of familiar beady eyes watching them particularly intently. The morning's gossip about these new arrivals had travelled quickly, and it was the news the smartly dressed man in the white suit had been waiting

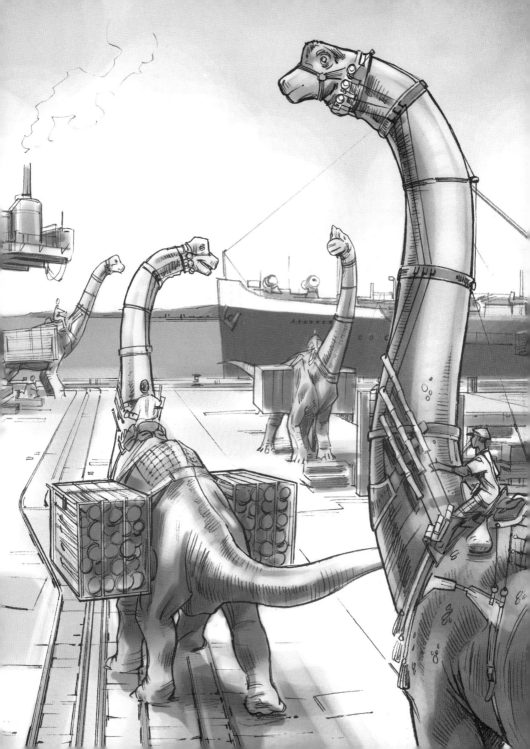

for. From where he was standing on the deck of a large cargo ship, he had a clear view of them: the ever-so-stuck-up Brownlee woman, Theodore Logan the do-gooder, little-brat Bea and the filthy saur boy who had his Beast on a rope like a pet. They were all in the perfect position for what he wanted – but his two henchmen weren't.

'Idiots!' he muttered angrily to himself.

He waved at them, at first just a small gesture, to avoid drawing attention to himself, but then a more exaggerated raising of his arms. Finally he caught their eye. He jerked a stubby finger towards Bea and the others, and then at one of the brachios, and mimed a hard punch.

The two men on the dock watched their boss's gesticulations. 'Guess we'd better get on with it before he gets angry,' muttered one.

They sidled over to the nearest brachio unloading crates, and climbed up the ladder attached to its leg. The men clambered along the saur's back until they were behind the driver, then one pulled out a cosh, and knocked the driver out with one swipe. A quick push, and the unconscious driver tumbled off the brachio and hit the dockside with a thump.

Carter and Buster turned at the same time. Sacks, crates and cases all make their own distinct sounds, and so does a body when it hits the ground. Carter couldn't see the source of the noise, but he was aware that something new had caught his tyrant's attention. Buster looked around, his nostrils quivering.

Shielding his eyes, Carter squinted up at a man in a white suit on the deck of a cargo ship opposite. He was standing in front of the bright morning sun, which was steadily rising. The man seemed to be looking straight at him. There was something strange and yet familiar about him, about his posture, but – because of the sun – Carter couldn't make him out clearly.

Ding-a-ling, ding, ding, ting-ting, ting-ting.

Bea looked back up at the nearest brachio, which now had two drivers working the command bells.

'Carter! Buster! Come on, we're heading off.'

Bea tugged at Carter's arm, but her brother didn't move – his gaze was fixed on the silhouetted figure.

'It's rude to stare, Carter. Come on, it's time to go.'

Carter gave a last look at the figure in the white suit. There was definitely something familiar about him, so he raised his hand and gently waved before following his sister.

Buster was also taking his time to be moved. Theodore tried to turn him but the tyrant's head was still craned around, its large nostrils scenting at the air. 'Someone's probably unloading a fishing boat,' he said grumpily. 'Come on, Buster. Stop thinking about your next meal all the time.' Theodore finally managed to pull the tyrant's head around, but in doing so it nudged Bunty, who dropped her umbrella to the ground. As she bent to pick it up, Buster trod on it.

'Move, you stupid lump!' said Bunty. She tried to push the tyrant's leg back up, but Buster was unsettled, jerking from side to side. His movement knocked Bunty off balance and to the ground. She grabbed hold of the tyrant's rope to haul herself up.

'Easy, Buster,' said Theodore, trying to calm the saur, but the huge beast was becoming so agitated Theodore knew he couldn't hold it for long. 'Carter!' he called.

A shadow passing over Bea's head made her look up.

The nearest brachio had swung suddenly to the left, then lurched back to the right. Loose straps swayed overhead like a pendulum. The large wooden container that had been strapped to its side looked unstable and gave a twisting creak. Carter suddenly let out a shrill whistle of alarm as the bars holding it in place gave way and sprung open.

The tyrant reacted immediately, leaping aside and yanking Bunty and Theodore with it, as the packing container smashed to the ground, sending splinters of wood and tins of crab pâté flying.

Carter and Bea dived for cover. The brachio lurched erratically around the dockside, dragging the remains of the crate, and spilling more of its contents all over the place.

Bea jumped up first. Theodore was tangled in the rope by the tyrant, but unhurt. Bunty, lying on the ground, looked stunned.

'Well, that was an accident waiting to happen.' Bea patted herself down. 'Honestly, who would let amateurs drive a brachio on a busy dock?' She suddenly realised she sounded like her grandmother.

Carter tugged at his sister and pointed to a slumped body on the ground. Bea looked at the unconscious man, then at the two drivers dismounting the large lurching brachiosaur.

'Hang on, they're not in uniform!' Bea said.

The two men were scarpering. Carter quickly looked around for the man in the white suit, but he'd vanished.

The brachio, with no driver to control it, was in a state of confusion. The sound of jingling bells ringing all around it sent it into a blind panic. Bea saw one of its huge feet about to stamp on the unconscious driver, and rushed to his aid, just managing to drag the man clear before the creature's foot came crashing down.

A dockhand ran to the brachio's back leg and started to climb its ladder, but was kicked back and sent tumbling. Another managed to climb up halfway, and attempted to cut the single red cord that led from the base of the brachio's tail to the top of its head and which acted as an emergency stop device, but one jerk from the brachio and he toppled off.

Bea and Carter both saw how they had been trying to reach the red cord, but no other dockworkers wanted to try to get near the saur. The ropes and winches still connected to the smashed container whipped left and right as the crazed brachio swished its head around.

Carter leapt into action. He ran to the saur and scuttled up it. Within moments he was on top of its back. He pulled one of the raptor claws from his waistband and slashed through the red cord. This immediately silenced the jangling bells that had been sending the saur berserk. Carter stepped up to its tree trunk of a neck and patted it. With silence at last, the brachio calmed down. Carter could feel its huge heart beating more slowly under his feet.

He looked down. The tackle and ropes were still bound to the creature. He climbed the rope ladder up the back of its neck. Halfway up it was twisted with the harness and the first part of the tackle. Carter looked down again to make sure that Bea was safely out of the way, before cutting it free.

With the brachio calm and the danger over, the people on the dock came out of hiding. The harbourmaster was the first to appear.

'I knew that dangerous tyrant should never have stepped foot on my dock!' he shouted angrily. 'Look what it's done! It scared my brachios and caused all this mess!' He looked up at Carter.

'And you, you filthy infested boat boy, what are you doing on my saur? Get down, I tell you, GET DOWN!'

Before anyone could reason with the red-faced man, who was stamping up and down in his anger, he trod on some of the splintered crate. Stepping back in agony, and with a loud curse, the harbourmaster slipped on a tin of crab pâté and tumbled over the side of the dock, straight into the cargo boat's dirty bilge water.

Two dockhands came to the aid of the now conscious but groggy driver. Carter slid down the brachio's neck and then climbed quickly down the ladder on its leg. He gave the brachio a pat, then darted off before the angry harbourmaster could climb back up onto the dock.

'Right – let's see how much trouble we can get into at the train station,' Theodore muttered. He hooked Bunty's arm around his, and quickly marched away from the chaotic scene.

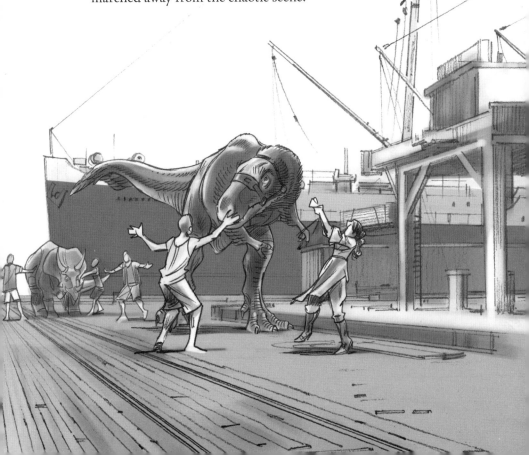

✦ ✦ ✦

The man in the white suit stepped down the gangway and straight over to where his two men were hiding behind a stacked pile of cargo.

'Job well done, eh, boss?' grinned one.

'And what job is that?' growled the man in the suit. 'I don't remember telling you to almost kill them.'

'But, boss, you ever driven a brachio before?' said the man defensively. 'It ain't easy. There are no instructions, just lots of strings to pull. I think we did quite well.'

'Oh you do, do you?' snarled the man. He swung back his white jacket to reveal his lethal bullhook. 'Ash, Bishop, I should have left you behind with the others to rot! You're both a liability. Tell me why I shouldn't hook you up by your eyelids and hang you out to dry!'

With that, Christian Hayter swung his bullhook. Alarmed, both men leapt back and it smashed into a barrel, water squirting out from the leak and soaking the men completely.

'Next time!' growled Hayter threateningly.

4

Mombasa Train Station

~ another problem to be paid for ~

The train station was just a short distance from the port. The railway line from Mombasa to Lake Victoria stretched deep into the heart of East Africa, and was the quickest way to make the long journey

to Nairobi, and then on by road to the Brownlee reserve.

Carter and Bea stayed outside the booking office with Buster, while Bunty and Theodore made the arrangements for their journey. Bea had been here before as a younger child and remembered clearly the smells and sounds and the wonder of the fresh air and open landscape from the train window. This would be their reward for enduring the long journey. Carter looked on in awe at the smoke-belching metal leviathan on the railway track. Bea could almost see his brain working it all out. Here he was, eleven years old and seeing a train for the first time. 'If only things had been different,' she said sadly. 'You would have had your own train set. I can imagine you opening it for your sixth birthday, having all the track laid out by lunchtime, and being told off for sneaking downstairs at night to play with it, too eager to sleep.' She felt wistful for all the years she had lost with her brother.

Inside the ticket office, Bunty and Theodore were finding that organising a livestock carriage for Buster meant yet more unavoidable hassle, rules and regulations.

'Rules are rules,' said the stationmaster. 'But new rules can be written … at an extra cost, naturally,' he went on, aware of the opportunity for a bonus to pad out his small pay packet.

A travel permit was agreed and carefully handwritten, but doubled in price when the stationmaster went outside and realised the tyrant in question was unfamiliar and only restrained by a rope with a small shaven-headed boy holding the other end.

Another problem emerged when it turned out the only available livestock carriage already held two allosaurs, destined to travel in the opposite direction. After some very long but fruitless discussions with their owner, Bunty quickly offered to purchase them at an inflated price from the less than friendly owner to resolve the matter.

'Always room for a few more at the lodge,' said Theodore. 'Besides, we've probably saved them from a grim end. Judging by their misaligned teeth, they're inbred. I suspect their final destination was a backyard butcher.'

♦ ♦ ♦

The crowd of onlookers made it easy for Christian Hayter to find who he was looking for, but difficult to do anything about it. He stood in the shadows of a corrugated-iron shed close to the engine, where he could just overhear the children's conversation without being seen. His moment would have to wait.

♦ ♦ ♦

Standing downwind, Carter froze to the spot as a smell wafted past him. It was hard to be certain, as there was a heady scent of everything imaginable going on in the station – food sellers, unusual livestock, fumes and many hot, perspiring people, all of which were new to his nose – but this particular smell stood out because it was familiar, and in a bad way. Hayter's white suit and hat could do a lot to disguise his appearance, but his body odour was unmistakable.

'Are you okay, Carter? You look like you've seen a ghost,' said Bea.

Carter looked puzzled. 'Ghost?'

Bea smiled. 'Sorry. "Seen a ghost" is just a phrase,' she explained. 'Like you've seen something bad.' She frowned, to show him 'bad'.

Carter nodded. 'Bad. Smell bad.' He wrinkled his nose and gave a scowl of disgust to show her he'd picked up something strong and unpleasant in the air. 'Bad ghost. Bad man. Here.' Carter looked around.

Bea laughed.

'Bad man … Hayter?' she said. 'Here? Impossible! Anyway, I doubt Mr Hayter is the only man who suffers from deeply offensive body odour.'

In the shadows, Hayter bridled as he eavesdropped.

'I'll show her deeply offensive body odour,' he growled.

'It's not your fault, boss,' murmured Ash. 'Thirty days at sea on a fishing boat is enough to make anyone stink.'

'Shut up!' snapped Hayter. 'Bishop, did you find out where they're going?'

Bishop smiled and produced three train tickets.

'We did indeed, boss.'

'Good.' Hayter nodded, taking the tickets. 'Then let's get on board.'

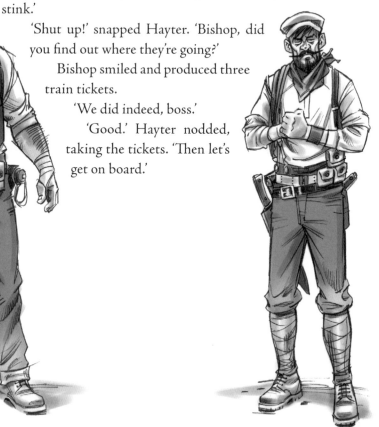

5

The View from the Train

~ standing room only ~

'I'm sorry, sir, third class is at the back.'

The conductor, swaying slightly with the movement of the train, studied the three tickets in his hand before giving them back to the man in the white suit and his two companions, and gestured down the carriages to the furthest door.

Christian Hayter stared at the conductor, then at the ticket in his hand. Ash and Bishop exchanged uncomfortable looks.

'Do I look like a third-class traveller?' Hayter demanded angrily.

'No, but these look like third-class tickets, and this is a first class carriage you are sitting in,' replied the conductor firmly.

Hayter now glared at the unhappy Ash and Bishop. He pulled his wallet from his pocket.

'All right. One first-class ticket for me. My servants will travel in the rear.'

The conductor shook his head.

'I'm sorry, sir, that won't be possible. The first-class carriage is full, and so is second class. As I've already said, your tickets are in third.'

'You mean I've got to sit on some hard wooden bench for the rest of the journey?' demanded Hayter.

'No, that won't be the case at all,' said the conductor. 'There are no reservations in third class, and the seats are already full. So it's standing room only.'

Hayter scowled. The conductor hurriedly offered another comment to make things better but inadvertently made it a million times worse. 'You could stay with the livestock who travel better than third class ... but today there is a tyrant aboard.'

Hayter stared at the man, stunned. But not wanting to draw undue attention to himself in such close quarters, he slowly stood up, barged his way past the conductor, and headed towards the next carriage, followed by Ash and Bishop.

'Sorry, boss,' muttered Ash nervously.

'I'll deal with you two later over this!' Hayter growled.

◆ ◆ ◆

Buster lay contentedly in the livestock carriage, taking in all the smells that came in through the vents in the wooden partitions. Suddenly the tyrant sat bolt upright. The door had swung open, and brought with it the smell of the tyrant's former master. The saur chattered its lower jaw with a rattle, as it breathed in slowly.

Hayter knew the sound well, and stopped.

'Keep moving!' came the cry from the conductor, closing the door on the passenger carriage behind him.

Hayter, fuming, marched onwards. The partition shook violently as the tyrant barged up close to it and let out a chilling roar. It scrabbled around till it found a missing panel, where it peered through at them with its caustic yellow eye.

Hayter unclipped his bullhook and dragged it along the partition wall and up to his Beast's eye. The curved, polished metal spike caught the strips of daylight that shone in through the many holes in the sides.

'Remember this, traitor?' he growled, his voice low and filled with menace.

The tyrant recoiled violently at the sight of it, startling the allosaurs.

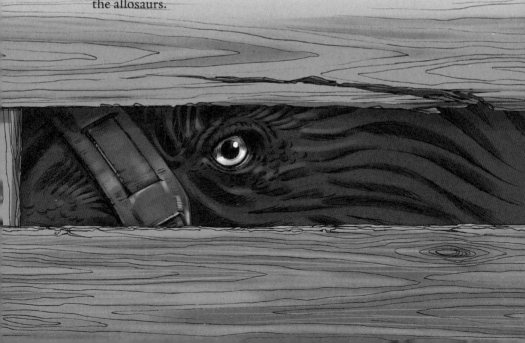

'I told you to move it!' The conductor pushed past Ash and Bishop, and shoved Hayter in the back.

This was the last straw for Hayter, who let his old self re-emerge from his new, gentrified white-suited persona. He swung at the conductor with his bullhook in rage, impaling the man's uniform cap onto the wooden partition with a splintering thud.

'Right, that's it!' shouted the conductor, as he beat a hasty retreat. 'You're off this train at the next stop!'

Luckily for him, it took Hayter a good tug to get the hook out of the wall before he could try for a second swing. But the tyrant was quicker off the mark. It tried to turn in the confined space and in doing so, thrashed the partition so hard it broke away at one end, trapping Hayter, Ash and Bishop in the walkway beside it.

Buster sent another chattering roar over the shattered mess, and the allosaurs jolted frantically. Ash pulled Hayter to his feet as the other end of the partition split away, sending Bishop to the floor again.

'Let's get out of here, boss,' said Ash urgently.

The conductor slammed the connecting door shut and they heard the bolt slide home, sealing off their route back to first class.

◆ ◆ ◆

The view from the train was amazing. Carter was glued to his window seat as he watched the African landscape open up before him. He had never been this far inland before. Since leaving Aru they had only docked in small ports near to lush coastline. Prior to this, his only home had been a dense rainforest where the sky was only visible directly above you in small pockets between the canopy of trees. Here, the sky was wide open, the top half hazy-blue and the lower a dusty beige. The trees were thin and scattered, leaving room for coarse grasses and bushes. Hidden in these lands was a whole host of new and exciting creatures to discover.

Bunty was also lost in reverie, looking at the once pristine landscape that had been farmed the same way for thousands of years. It was rapidly changing now. New crops were harvested with heavy machinery for a Western diet of oil, gold and diamonds, and the workforce came cheap. As they wound their way inland, signs of the new emerging economy were plain to see.

Bea unfolded a pocket map that Bunty had bought, and tried her best to pick up where she'd left off in her last geography lesson on board the *Orca* using Captain Woods' nautical charts. She located where they were and pointed to it.

'We are here.' To make sure Carter understood her, she pointed outside the carriage and then tapped on the map again. 'Here.'

He nodded.

Bea ran her finger along the train line. 'We go on the train to here.'

Carter looked up, pulled on an imaginary steam whistle, and let out a perfect rendition of it that turned everyone's head.

They were interrupted by the appearance of the train conductor, out of breath, hatless and in a state of panic.

'Excuse me, I'm so sorry to bother you, but we have an issue in the livestock carriage.' He gulped for breath, then burst out in a low and urgent whisper, desperate not to alarm the other passengers: 'Your saurs are loose!'

'What?' Theodore exclaimed, horrified. He leapt up and tapped Carter on the arm. 'Come on, lad, we have work to do!'

◆ ◆ ◆

Hayter's white suit was not looking its best. Most of the people here in third class were women with babies, and old people. It seemed, from the sight of the legs dangling past the glassless windows, that all the men and children were riding on top of the train.

'Right, we'll go up on the roof,' said Hayter.

'The roof?' echoed Bishop apprehensively.

'Well, we can't get back through to first class any other way!' snapped Hayter. With that, he climbed determinedly out of the window and hauled himself up.

◆ ◆ ◆

Theodore unbolted the thick door that led into the livestock carriage, and he and Carter stepped inside.

'I can't afford to leave it unlocked!' said the nervous conductor, and he bolted the door shut behind them.

'Great!' muttered Theodore acidly.

The allosaurs had herded themselves into a corner of the shattered partition at the far end, doing their best to keep as far away from the threatening tyrant as possible. The tyrant stood its ground in the middle of the carriage, snorting angrily, and every now and then it crashed its huge forehead into the floor, or rammed the walls.

'What's upset him?' asked Theodore, bewildered.

Carter sniffed the air, then said, 'Bad man.'

Theodore looked at him, puzzled.

There was an angry bellow from the tyrant. It flicked its massive tail, smashing a hole in the carriage's wall; splinters of broken wood hurtled in all directions. The allosaurs squealed at the far end of the carriage, pushing against one another so much that Theodore saw there was a danger of one crushing the other.

'Carter, we have to calm Buster down,' Theodore said urgently. 'If we don't, he'll wreck the carriage, and the whole train could come off the rails. Hundreds of people would be killed!'

Carter turned towards the tyrant and gently blew out a long breath. At the same time, the boy extended his arms wide to either side, then gently let them slowly down, and slowly up again. Carter moved nearer to the tyrant one tiny pace at a time, his arms moving slowly up and down, as if he still had his feathered wings – and all the time he breathed in, then out, a long breath each time; letting his scent drift towards the agitated saur.

Theodore saw the tyrant calm down gradually. Its tail stopped swinging, its great head stopped moving from side to side, its enormous mouth with rows of vicious teeth began to close, and its breathing slowed …

✦ ✦ ✦

It was like a small town on the roof of third class, with men and boys clustered together. Those who had got on board first had managed to get a place next to the beaded rail that ran the length of the train's roof, giving them something to hold on to, or to hook a leg around. Those who had a place further towards the centre of the roof, with no handholds, tended to slide whenever the train went around a curve in the tracks, sliding back again as the train straightened its course. The appearance of the scowling and muscular Hayter, in his now crumpled white suit, along with thug-like Ash and Bishop, had caused momentary consternation among those crammed on the train roof. They seemed to think this might be some action on the behalf of the railway company – that the three men had come to deal with them, possibly even throw them off the train, after assuming people might be travelling without tickets.

Hayter strode along the roof of the train, the bullhook dangling ominously from his powerful right fist. One look at the determination of his stride – even as the train rocked from side to side – and the grim scowl on his face, and the men and boys on the roof scuttled out of his way. Ash and Bishop followed, but at a slower and warier pace, doing their best to keep their balance on the moving vehicle.

'If you ask me, the boss is losing it,' muttered Ash. 'One minute he's saying we've got to keep away from the targets, and now he's going looking for them!'

'Don't let him hear you say that,' Bishop murmured back.

Ahead of them, Hayter had stopped, and seemed to be listening intently.

'What's up, boss?' asked Ash.

'Ssssh!' said Hayter. He looked along the train. 'Where are we, do you reckon?'

'Somewhere on the roof of the livestock carriage, I think,' said Bishop.

Hayter dropped to his hands and knees, and pressed his ear to the wood of the roof. Ash and Bishop exchanged glances, then reluctantly got down on their knees and copied him, as the roof rocked and rolled.

◆ ◆ ◆

Theodore watched Carter, marvelling at his talent. He had brought the tyrant under control with only gentle breaths, and without brutality. It was visibly calming.

Then the tyrant suddenly came out of its reverie; tail swinging, huge mouth agape, eyes fixed on the ceiling of the carriage.

Carter leapt back. Buster had snapped back into a rage.

RRRRAWRRRRR!!!!

The allosaurs, who had calmed down when the tyrant did, began to panic again, shrieking and shoving and crashing into one another.

'Bad man smell!' shouted Carter to Theodore. 'He angry!'

❖ ❖ ❖

Up on the roof, Hayter smiled as he heard the tremendous roar beneath them.

'That's my Beast!' he smirked. 'And now's the time for—'

But Ash and Bishop never found out what it was time for, because at that second the roof beneath them erupted upwards, as if there'd been an explosion in the carriage below, and the tyrant's massive head burst out through the roof; mouth agape and jaws slavering. All three men flung themselves, in panic, towards the edge of the moving train …

6

Nairobi Polo Club

~ playing catch-up with a tyrant ~

T he never-ending landscape and train line consumed the best part of two days but finally they had come to their stop. A car was waiting at Nairobi train station, the driver holding a sign for the Brownlee party. A trailer was also waiting, with a handler who took the reins of the two allosaurs. There was a slight delay to their onward travel while Bunty settled up the damages to the livestock carriage with yet another official. Once Buster had smashed his head out of the top of the carriage, the tyrant had calmed down and the train journey had passed relatively uneventfully, although Buster had travelled all the rest of the way with his head poking through the roof of the carriage, like a dog with its head hanging out of the window of a car. Carter had climbed up and stayed with him, to share the better view and avoid more of Bea's lessons.

Theodore concluded that the tyrant must have been agitated at being shut up inside in an unfamiliar place. So rather than restrain Buster again, Carter was allowed –

happily – to ride behind the car on his tyrant's back. Soon a game emerged, in which Buster would run right up behind the car, close enough to dip his face into the back seat, whereupon Bea patted the tyrant on the nose. Then Buster would slow, drop back and trail far behind, out of the dust of the car, only to repeat the sequence over and over. Upon arrival at the grand entrance to Nairobi Polo Club, the driver, somewhat shaken, forced a smile as he held the car door open for Bunty.

'Excellent driving,' Bunty told him as she stepped out. 'Was that the first time you have played catch-up with a tyrant?'

'No, madam – the last time it was with an angry Horned Tyrant, and he ate the spare tyre.'

Theodore grabbed the cases and grinned at the driver. 'Don't worry, old chap, you survived. Well done!'

The clean, white building of the polo club shone in the afternoon sunshine. Smartly dressed people milled about, and there was the faint sound of classical music in the air. For Bunty it was like heaven, the polar opposite of the drab poverty and dirt of the previous days' travels and the repetitive clattering of train wheels beneath them.

Buster too felt at home straight away. A water feature outside, with lush flowers and lily pads, attracted his attention. Carter dismounted in one move as Buster dipped his head under and resurfaced with a large lily pad atop his head. The tyrant gurgled with delight. Carter

burst out laughing and flopped in to join him for a cool dip, completely unaware of the uniformed doormen who were aghast at the unconventional sight and clearly had no idea what to do with it.

Bea, Bunty and Theodore walked up the steps of the magnificently decorated entrance to the club. A heavily bearded Indian man wearing a magnificent turban waited to greet them.

'Bunty, this is indeed travelling light!' boomed the man. 'One car? I never imagined it was this bad.'

'Ranjit Bapat, my dear friend!' Bunty was delighted to see him. 'As you can see from our bedraggled state, it's even worse than that – but everything is fine now, seeing you here. Tell me you received my telegrams?'

'Yes, indeed. Your new trunks arrived from England only last week and are already in your favourite room.'

Theodore strode up and exchanged a firm handshake with the man.

'I trust you also got my telegram, old friend?' he said.

Ranjit smiled.

'No telegram was needed to alert me of your needs, Mr Logan. There is a bottle in your room, waiting for you, next to a bucket of ice.'

'Thank you,' Theodore grinned. 'I could certainly do with a drink.'

'And perhaps a bath?' suggested Ranjit with a tactful smile.

Theodore laughed. 'Agreed!' He took a deep sniff of his stained clothes. 'It's been a long journey.'

Ranjit turned to Bea, and held out his hands.

'Now, this cannot be the little Bea I know so well. You must be her long-lost older sister!'

Bea smiled, and ran to him for a big hug.

'You're close to the truth.' She pulled away with a happy smile. 'Ranj, may I introduce my long-lost little brother, Carter Kingsley.'

Bea turned to find Carter was not by her side but frolicking with Buster in the pond. She poked two fingers in the corners of her mouth and whipped up a shrill whistle, which caught their attention. With a wave Carter bounded over, dripping wet. Bunty frowned at both her grandchildren.

Ranjit looked at the scruffy urchin with the shaven head, blinked, and then laughed out loud.

'Ha, that's almost believable! Your friend does indeed have your father's blue eyes, Bea,' he said. 'But who is this really?'

In chorus, Theodore, Bunty and Bea all said together: 'Carter Kingsley!'

For the first time, the owner of the polo club was speechless. Ranjit held his hands over his mouth, dropped to his knees and held his arms open. Carter, copying Bea, ran up and gave the stranger a great big hug.

'Oh my dear boy, where on earth have you been hiding?' said Ranjit. He hugged the boy, then said: 'You must explain in full, but later. I know your grandmother and Theodore don't want to wait in my club reception for a moment longer. Shall we tell them to go away to their rooms, while you and I head to the stables, Carter, with that fine-looking steed of yours?'

'It's a Black Dwarf Tyrant,' said Bea.

'He Buster,' Carter chirped up.

'And a rarity in these parts,' added Ranjit, smiling. 'Well, I bet Buster is hungry, and, like Theo, could obviously do with a good soak as well.'

With that, Ranjit put his arms around Bea and Carter, and walked them towards what was left of the ornate pond.

Bunty called after her grandchildren, 'Don't be too long. Drinks before dinner are at six o'clock sharp. Don't be late!'

She smiled at Theodore as they walked inside. 'It feels great to be back!'

7

Even More Impossible

~ such a friendly tyrant ~

anjit was keen to hear Carter's story, as they walked Buster towards the polo ground.

'You must tell me all about yourself, my boy,' he invited.

Unable to understand, Carter looked to Bea for help.

'I'm afraid he's been away from human society for a

long time,' explained Bea. 'He hasn't yet properly grasped our speech.'

'Ah.' Ranjit nodded, and smiled. 'In that case, I will tell him about myself and how I came to be here. It may provoke some words from him, you never know. Questions.'

'I doubt it,' murmured Bea, but she knew from experience that once Ranjit was in full flow it was difficult to stop him.

'I originally hail from Baroda in western India, and knew your grandfather Sidney well. Together we imported used steam trains from India to Kenya. Most of them did not last long because of the new tracks. You can't just cut a line across the land and expect it to stay there.

The earth moves, and with it the metal tracks.'

'Trains,' explained Bea to Carter, and made a train noise, which Carter repeated with a nod to show he understood.

'All the first trains derailed within a year,' continued Ranjit. 'Building railways is expensive and you can waste a lot of money on new trains, so we sold cheap, used ones, and lots of them.

'After that, we imported allosaurs. Your grandfather had already set up a stud farm in America, where your dear mother, Grace, met Franklin Kingsley. I started this club and introduced allo-polo to Africa, so we could have a good old game of chukkas with the saurs.'

Carter looked helplessly at Bea, not understanding what Ranjit was saying, but Bea just shook her head and smiled.

'Later, Sidney and Barbara bought their land five hours west from here, to build a reserve. How long has it been since you were last there, Beatrice?'

'Too long, Ranj,' said Bea. 'I can't wait to show Carter all the wildlife. He's curious to learn everything.'

'It looks like he already knows how to ride. When did he start to learn?'

'About two months ago,' said Bea. 'Buster used to be called the Beast. He'd been trained by a really nasty man, the hard way, and was forced to attack us. Somehow Carter befriended Buster, and now they are inseparable.'

'A boy and a Black Dwarf Tyrant as friends ...' Ranjit shook his head in awed amazement. 'That is incredible!' 'That's only the most recent part of the story, Ranj. Until we found him, Carter had not spoken to another human or lived with any. He was raised by shadow raptors on a remote island.'

Ranjit shook his head again.

'Yesterday, I would have sworn on my life that it was impossible that the son of Franklin Kingsley would ride into my club bareback on a Black Tyrant, yet today it has happened. But, sometimes, the more unbelievable a story, the more it becomes believable. Look at all the world's religious stories, myths and legends. Perhaps the impossible is possible!'

He opened up the enclosure gate to lead Buster towards a stable, but suddenly the tyrant stopped and let out a low growl, much to the alarm of the other riders, who were preparing their prize allosaurs for the afternoon match.

A bell rang out.

'It's time for the remaining players to get on the pitch; the game is about to start,' explained Ranjit. He gestured. 'Come on – quickly, Carter – it looks like your tyrant's making the allosaurs jumpy.'

But Buster had other plans. Flaring his nostrils, he turned towards the allosaurs as their players mounted them. Carter could tell something was up, and knew this was not the place to get into trouble again. He tugged at Buster's head, but something had caught the tyrant's full attention.

A group of riders had gathered to ride out onto the pitch, and their allosaurs were becoming agitated as the tyrant took a step closer towards them. 'Easy,' murmured Bea.

She reached up to pat Buster's muzzle, but suddenly the tyrant lunged at the allosaurs, scattering them. One allosaur bucked its rider, who slipped to the ground. In a panic, the allosaur scrambled upright in a tangle of reins, as the tyrant pinned its rider to the floor with a large foot. The other allosaurs bolted in all directions, adding to the confusion.

Ranjit jumped in and, together with Bea, pulled hard on Buster's rope, trying to restrain him.

'Do something, Carter!' Bea cried out.

Carter jumped down from Buster's back and stood in front of the tyrant. The creature tried to nudge Carter away with its muzzle, but Carter hissed loudly and slapped Buster sharply on the snout. This was enough to get the saur's full attention, and Carter commanded him to sit.

The tyrant stepped back from the fallen rider, and sat down.

'I'm so sorry!' Bea said, as she and Ranjit rushed to the rider's aid. 'He's normally such a friendly tyrant.'

The shaking man sat up, dazed. Totally embarrassed,

Ranjit led the man away, apologising profusely.

But the commotion was far from over.

'Restrain that allosaur, before it bites someone!' came a cry from the polo ground.

The riderless allosaur had bolted onto the pitch and was lashing out at the people trying to regain control of it. One unfortunate handler managed to get hold of the reins, but was dragged along the ground as the frightened creature circled round and round in a panic.

'Stay!' Carter ordered Buster, realising he had to help the frightened allosaur.

As Carter ran off, Bea crossed her arms and stood directly in front of Buster, looking firmly into the tyrant's yellow eyes.

'Yes, you naughty boy! Sit there and don't move!'

Carter ran towards the terrified allosaur, which was now dragging a second person behind it from a lasso around its neck. Its strong tail swished over the heads of the people trying to control it, making it impossible for them to stand up, but by hanging on for dear life they were attempting to slow it down enough for a third person to try where they had failed.

The allosaur started to buck, and whipped the first handler into the air. As he was forced to let go, the allosaur gained more momentum, and rid itself of the second handler as well.

All this time, Carter slowly positioned himself. The

terrified allosaur was circling in a panic. One of its blinkers had wedged forward, limiting the sight from its left eye.

On its next lap, Carter calmly stepped forward, raised his arm and grabbed hold of the allosaur's neck feathers, lifting his feet and letting the allosaur pull him off the ground as it swept by. With perfect timing and precision, Carter flew in an arc and landed astride the saur, just in front of the slipped saddle and behind the creature's shoulders. Gripping tightly, he grabbed its reins and brought the allosaur under control.

As it slowed, Carter bent forward and ran his hands along its neck, towards its head, then back down again, in a long stroking motion. The allosaur raised its head high to the sky and then gracefully lowered itself. With the saur calm, Carter dismounted. He moved in front of it and continued to stroke his hands up and down a few more times, before finally holding onto its muzzle, lowering its head to the floor and patting it, until it was lying down, completely still.

Everyone was silent, too mesmerised to say anything.

Ranjit ran over, gesturing in astonishment.

'I have never seen anything like this! It is impossible! How on earth did you do that?'

Carter had no trouble understanding Ranjit's meaning. He gave a small smile, and shrugged. Then the fallen rider appeared from behind Ranjit, and the smile disappeared from Carter's face.

'Sorry,' apologised Carter who was getting quite used to saying the word.

The rider lifted his helmet.

'Sorry? Sorry?' The rider shook his head and smiled. 'Gracious me, it's absolutely not your fault, my boy.'

Carter looked up. 'No sorry?'

'No, not at all! Thank you, more like! Thank you so much!' He put his hands on Carter's shoulders. 'Thank you for saving my allosaur. He is very expensive, and normally in that state there is only one way to stop a rampaging saur: shoot it.' He smiled again. 'I'm Lambert Knútr. And who are you?'

'His name is Carter,' Bea chipped in from behind them. 'Please forgive him, he talks very little.'

Lambert looked around. 'And who are you, young lady?'

'Beatrice. I'm his big sister,' she announced proudly.

'Well, he may not talk that much, but he knows how to calm an allosaur. Was that your tyrant in the enclosure?'

Bea blushed. 'Oh gosh, yes. I'm so sorry for what Buster did. Are you hurt?'

'Just a few bruises,' he replied. 'Not many people survive a tyrant attack, so, again, I have to thank you for that.' Lambert Knútr smiled at Carter. 'I will be for ever in your debt.'

8

Hassler De Bois

~ *the disappearing Queen of Diamonds* ~

The gong struck six. Bunty stood by the bar in the gallery, looking at the door and wondering what was keeping the others. Drinks before dinner were at six; that was the rule at the polo club, and it needed to be adhered to. She had made herself perfectly clear.

'Good evening,' said a voice beside her. 'I don't believe we have had the pleasure?'

A large, portly man had sidled to the stool next to her, and was leaning on the bar, a drink in his hand.

'I'm Hassler De Bois,' he smiled, revealing a diamond inlaid into one of his front teeth.

Bunty had bumped into many men like this Hassler De Bois over the years – bores who haunted the bars of the world's top hotels and clubs. Still, she decided, we're all guests here. One can't be rude.

'Barbara Brownlee,' she responded. 'Pleased to meet you.'

'Brownlee ... widow of the late Sidney Brownlee?'

'That's correct.' Bunty nodded.

'Well, then you must have heard of me. De Bois of De Bois Diamonds?'

Bunty shook her head. 'No, I'm sorry.'

'I'm your new neighbour,' said De Bois. 'I own the old Keat estate next to yours.'

'I didn't know that,' Bunty replied with surprise. 'How did this come about? I'm very fond of Mr Keat. Is he well?'

De Bois shrugged.

'No idea. Not seen him since I took over. He got into some financial difficulty, and I offered him a good price for his land.'

'He must have been heartbroken; he loved that estate,' said Bunty.

De Bois ignored this.

'Can I get you a drink?' he asked, clicking his fingers at the barman.

Bunty shook her head.

'No, thank you. I'm waiting for my guests.'

'I hear you refuse to issue hunting permits on your place,' said De Bois. 'One thing I have to ask: how do you turn a profit?'

Bunty hesitated, not really wanting to get involved in an in-depth conversation about her estate, and desperately wishing that Theodore, Bea and Carter would hurry up. Fortunately for her, before she could reply, De Bois made a bold proposition.

'Actually, I'm keen to expand my estate,' he said. 'Are you thinking of selling?'

Bunty looked at him in shock.

'Absolutely not,' she said firmly. 'I couldn't possibly let the place go. My dear late husband Sidney bought that land many years ago from the government, when he found out they were going to force the local farmers and tribes from their homes, flatten it for wheat fields and drain the natural springs to water it. Sidney loved that place and he is buried there, and one day I wish to rest next to him for ever.'

'But it's just scrubland with rocks,' De Bois protested.

'It may be that to you, but to the wildlife it's home, and that's exactly how it will stay.'

De Bois looked as if he was going to press his case further, but suddenly he switched on a smile and nodded. 'Well. Each to their own, dear lady, that's my philosophy.'

A movement near the door caught Bunty's eye, and with relief she saw that her family had finally arrived. The sight of her grandchildren filled her with joy. Bea looked as ladylike as Bunty had always wished her to be. Carter was almost unrecognisable in a smart jacket and tie, despite his convict haircut. Theodore, too, was literally a changed man, cleanly shaved with slicked hair and sparkling eyes, wearing a white tuxedo with black bow tie.

De Bois gave a broad smile as they approached.

'Looks like your guests are here, Mrs Brownlee,' he said. 'Hello! I'm Hassler De Bois.'

'Logan, Theodore Logan,' said Theodore, taking the man's sweaty hand and receiving a limp handshake.

De Bois turned to Bea and Carter, producing a pack of cards from his pocket.

'How about a card trick, children? Pick any card.'

'Yes, do let Mr De Bois entertain you while we arrange our table,' said Bunty. 'This way, Theodore.'

As Bunty hustled Theodore away, she muttered, 'Let's make sure we are seated as far away as possible from that ghastly man. What took you so long?'

'Shoes,' replied Theodore.

'What, you forgot how to tie your laces?'

'No, Carter's shoes. It's his first time wearing them.'

Bunty nodded.

'Yes, bless him. He looks wonderful – I'm glad the clothes fit. Although that haircut suited him better when he was in rags. And you look smart, for a change.'

'Thanks, Bunty.' Theodore grinned. 'I'll try to not make a habit of it.'

◆ ◆ ◆

'So now you've signed your name on your card, and I have no way of knowing which one it is,' said De Bois, taking his pen back from Bea.

'Correct,' she replied, holding the card tightly to her chest. Carter was watching on with interest.

De Bois fanned out the pack of cards in a fancy way, impressing Carter, who'd never even seen a whole pack of cards before. The single card he owned, kept in his tin of worldly possessions that he had carried with him from Aru, came from a set. Carter was astonished and delighted to discover this. The portly gentleman reshuffled the pack and fanned them out again.

'Now put your card back in anywhere.' He turned his head away. 'I'm not looking.'

Bea did as instructed. De Bois confidently shuffled the pack for a third time, cut it, then tapped the top card.

'Pick it up.'

Bea lifted the top card and looked at it.

'Let me guess ... your card is the ... queen of diamonds?'

'Yes, my card is ...'

Bea turned her card around.

'... but this is the seven of spades.'

'Oh no, it can't be ...' De Bois was flustered. 'Where has the queen of diamonds gone?'

Bea and Carter exchanged looks.

De Bois continued to rummage through the pack.

'It's not here; it must have ...'

Bea and Carter did their best to stop themselves sniggering, as the trick disintegrated in front of them.

'It reminds me of the story of the disappearing Queen of Diamonds,' said De Bois with a heavy sigh. 'Have you heard it?'

'No,' Bea said, wanting to distract De Bois from the failure of his trick.

'It's a true story. A long time ago there was a diamond rush in these parts, caused by a crazy old man,' De Bois told them. 'He was lost and sheltered in a cave from a storm, and found that it was dripping with diamonds. They were so big he couldn't lift them. He had no equipment to mine them, and no way of carrying them all back. So the old man filled his pockets with as many of the stones scattered around the floor as possible. After the storm had passed, he headed out to find his way home. He planned to sell the loose diamonds, and buy new equipment and carts so that he could come back and excavate the cave. But he had no way of mapping where he was. The only thing he had to draw on was a pack of playing cards.'

De Bois held out his pack of cards dramatically.

'So he jotted down some notes on one card, and kept it safe. Then he left a trail, with the other cards wedged between rocks, so he could find his way back.'

He dealt out all the cards, one by one, into a loose pile onto the bar. Carter looked on, not following the story, but mesmerised still by the cards. Bea listened politely.

'After he'd used the other fifty-one cards, and both the jokers, he was still not in sight of home. So he started to leave diamonds from his pockets to mark the trail. Naturally he used the smallest first, and then the medium-sized ones, till he only had the big ones left. Before he knew it he was down to his last diamond, and it was the biggest of the lot. Huge, it was. He could not bear to leave it behind.'

Hassler paused and looked at Bea, who was now hanging on his every word.

'Well, what did he do?' she asked.

'Nothing. Years later, a young lad found a skeleton while playing out in the bush. He told his father, who went out to bury it properly. In the pocket of the skeleton's jacket was one playing card with some notes written on it, and in its clenched fist was a huge diamond.'

De Bois held up his clenched fist.

'He had to break the finger bones one by one to get it.'

And with that, he prised open his fingers to reveal a big boiled sweet in middle of his sweaty palm. He offered it to Bea, who hesitated, then politely took it but cringed at where it had just been.

'Anyway,' continued De Bois, 'when the man traded in the diamond, he refused to say how he had come by it. This got people suspicious. With his new wealth, the man hired a small army of strong men, bought lots of carts and loaded ankylos with new mining equipment. But before he got to set off he was killed in a bar brawl, and the notes describing the cave and trail were discovered written on the remaining card, the queen of diamonds.

'Everyone who could went looking for the cave filled with diamonds. People from all over, far and wide, heard of the story and rushed to these parts, looking for their fortune. Some claimed to have found part of the diamond trail, others said they had found playing cards blowing about in the wind.' De Bois gestured at his pack of cards. 'Of course, there are lots of small caves around here and every one of them was opened up, but no one found the cave dripping with diamonds, though many people lost their lives and squandered their savings looking for it. Eventually everyone gave up, and the mystery of the Queen of Diamonds faded away.'

'It sounds like it was just a hoax,' said Bea.

'It could have been,' said De Bois, nodding. 'But then this turned up.' He pulled out his wallet and from it took a playing card, which he handed to Bea.

'The queen of diamonds – with my signature on it!' Bea said in amazement. 'How did you do that?'

Carter took the card from her and examined it, then picked up the rest of the pack from the bar, and tried to fan them out.

'Keep them, boy,' said De Bois, grinning. 'Can't use them now that one is spoiled.' He seemed delighted by the children's amazement.

'Mr De Bois, up to your old tricks again, eh?'

Ranjit appeared with a smile, Bunty and Theodore behind him.

'Please excuse me, Beatrice and Carter,' Ranjit continued. 'You have been asked for by a guest who requests the pleasure of your company at dinner. If you don't mind following me?'

'So, alas, it seems I won't have your company,' said De Bois with a theatrical sigh. 'But don't forget what I said, Mrs Brownlee. When you're ready to sell your land, come to me. It would be my pleasure to purchase it from you.'

As Bunty, Theodore, Bea and Carter headed towards the dining room, Ranjit enquired quietly, 'What was all that about, Barbara, if you don't mind my asking?'

'Nothing,' said Bunty firmly.

'Good. Hassler De Bois is a horrible man,' murmured Ranjit. 'We call him "Piggy De Boy".'

Bunty shot a quick glance back towards the bar, and decided that Ranjit was right: De Bois' red, puffed-up cheeks and fat upward lips made him look almost pig-like, and to make matters worse his ears were longer than usual and hung off his head limply.

'If you take my advice, I'd do my best to avoid him,' continued Ranjit.

'He did entertain the children,' said Bunty.

'Don't be fooled,' said Ranjit. 'He's done that same card trick hundreds of times. It's to win people over. We believe that De Bois conned Michael Keat out of his estate in a rigged card game.'

'That's awful!' said Bunty, shocked. 'Why would he do that?'

'As you know, Keat was always in need of money, and he got desperate.'

'But how did he lose his estate in a card game?'

'Who knows, but you've seen how skilled De Bois is with sleight of hand. No one here will play cards with him because he always wins.'

'Do you know what happened to poor Michael Keat?' asked Bunty.

'When I saw him last, he was too upset to say anything. De Bois was with him. Made him pack up, hand over the estate and he was never seen again.'

'What does De Bois want with it? The land isn't valuable.'

'Apparently Michael Keat had travelled to Mombasa to trade in his last asset: a large, uncut diamond. That's where we think he met De Bois, whose diamond business is based there. Some people think that De Bois believes the diamond was found on Keat's estate. Since he got here he's been opening up all the old caves.' Ranjit looked seriously at Bunty. 'As I said, I warn you, as a friend, Bunty: be very careful of him.'

9

Lamprecht Knútr

~ *with the deep scar* ~

Ranjit lead the group into the grand dining room and to a large table, where a tall, handsome man with a deep scar running down one cheek was standing by the open fireplace.

'Mrs Barbara Brownlee, Mr Lamprecht Knútr.'

'Good evening. I am so pleased to be in your company.' The man bowed, then stepped forward and took Bunty's hand to kiss. 'Please call me Lambert. I prefer the English way of saying Lamprecht. I think it best to distance myself from my Prussian heritage. They were on the other side in the war.'

'Very well, Lambert. Please call me Barbara. I believe you have already met Beatrice and Carter.'

Lambert smiled at the children.

'Yes, and a good evening to you, Beatrice and Carter. You both look extremely elegant this evening.'

'Logan, Theodore Logan.' Theodore put out his hand and in return, to his pleasure, received a firm handshake.

'Good to meet you, Mr Logan. Mr Bapat has told me

you're a fine allo-polo player. Would you care to join us for a game tomorrow?'

Theodore smiled.

'Thank you for the invitation,' he replied warmly, 'but perhaps next time. We have to head off tomorrow. I am sorry that our tyrant stepped out of line ... and on you, this afternoon. I do hope you weren't hurt?'

Lambert winked at Carter.

'Fortunately, this brave young man saw that I wasn't.' He gestured at the table. 'I do hope you will join me for dinner. Eating by oneself can be quite lonely.'

They took their seats, and it was soon apparent that Lambert was a well-mannered host, listening to their stories and adding a few about his own exploits, but with modesty, Bea noticed, not in a boastful way.

Carter tried to follow what was being said, but without many hand gestures he soon became confused. Besides, his feet ached in the tight shoes.

Lambert ensured the topics of conversation were fun and interesting for Bea, so that she could contribute and laugh along to what was turning out to be very interesting evening. Both Carter and Bea kept staring at his scar, but dared not ask how he got it, in fear of turning the conversation down a darker path.

Lambert nodded towards Carter. 'He is quite a talented chap. Did you teach him how to ride an allosaur, Theodore?'

Theodore shook his head.

'He's been raised in Australia, picked a few tricks up from the local aborigines, I believe. We're just getting to know him,' replied Theodore. 'Sadly, his parents passed away, and I'm taking him back to England. He's a little behind on schoolwork, but I am sure we can sort all that out.'

This cover story had been discussed on the boat in great detail. The truth was so extraordinary that to outsiders it would sound like a fairy tale. Something more understandable had been concocted to explain Carter's lack of language and strange manners, and to avoid him being ridiculed for being feral.

Bunty had tried to teach Carter table manners, so that he could fit into polite society. Hot food had taken a while for him to get used to, but Carter had learnt that his hand was not the best thing to scoop it up with. He was still baffled by the variety of foods, and the various ways to eat. When the soup arrived, Bea saw Carter frowning as he studied the range of cutlery before him. She edged her chair closer to his, picked up the soup spoon and passed it to him, before their grandmother could notice.

'And what is it that you do, Lambert?' asked Bunty.

'Shipping, mostly. I inherited a small family business, a title, and lots of work, which I try to get other people to do for me. My time is better spent investing the family wealth into charitable projects.'

'That's very good of you,' said Bunty, impressed. 'I, too, have been trying to put my wealth to good use. I inherited an estate five hours drive from here. Our aim is to protect some of the remaining wildlife for the next generations, as everyone else seems to be set on killing it all off.'

'That sounds wonderful!' said Lambert, smiling. 'I was thinking about going on a jaunt, and was going to ask Ranjit where might be a good place to visit.'

'In that case, you must come to our lodge. Ranjit can organise transport for you.'

'How very kind of you.' Lambert picked up his napkin and dabbed his lips. 'Tell me of the wildlife at your reserve. Are there any interesting saurs?'

Bea was happy to join in at this. 'All the regulars,' she said proudly. 'Red Stytops, Thinhorn Tritops. A few types of krynos, you know, the ones with the shoulder spikes. Appatos wander in all the time and oh, there are White Titan Tyrants!'

'It sounds fascinating! I must come and visit. No stegs?'

Bunty nodded. 'The Steggi territory runs just to the west, about a day or two away. They are a nomadic tribe who live alongside the stegs in harmony with them. Find the Steggi, and you will find the mighty stegs. Theodore would be delighted show you everything.'

Theodore nodded.

'It will be my pleasure,' he said.

'In that case, I must definitely visit!' Lambert smiled. 'It sounds like paradise!'

The evening was a thrill, but it was getting late. Time had whizzed past with tricks, thrilling stories, great conversation and wonderful food, but now it was time for bed.

'We have an early start, if we're to avoid the heat of the day,' Bunty explained to Lambert.

Another early start, thought Bea ruefully. But this time her bedroom at the safari lodge would be waiting at the end of it.

◆ ◆ ◆

Christian Hayter was already fuming with anger as he mounted the steps of the Nairobi Polo Club, only to find his way barred by a large man wearing a smart uniform.

'Can I help you, sir?' asked the man, looking Hayter up and down.

Hayter's once immaculate white suit was no longer a suit, nor was it white. It had splinters of wood, rips and stains from his travels inside the train. Soot, dust and a multitude of splatted bugs also covered it from travelling on the outside of the train. His hair was greasy, and his chin stubbly and unshaven.

'I'm here to see someone,' snapped Hayter.

'Who?' demanded the man.

'That's none of your business,' snarled Hayter, and went to push past, but the man blocked his way.

'The Nairobi Polo Club is for its members and approved guests only. I am afraid you are neither, and I must ask you to leave.'

'Oh you must, must you?' growled Hayter. He glared at the doorman. 'Since I've been on this godforsaken continent I've been treated like dirt. I've been kicked out of my rightful first-class seat on a train. I've been sneered at and humiliated. I've been attacked. And I am fed up with it!'

The doorman returned Hayter's angry glare with a bland stare of his own.

'I'm sorry to hear that, sir. But if you don't leave, I shall call security and have you thrown out of the polo club grounds.'

'Really?' said Hayter, his temper now taking him over the edge. He thrust his face aggressively into the other man's. 'Do you know who I am?'

'No,' the man replied curtly.

Hayter grinned.

'Good,' he said.

With that, he swung a punch that knocked the doorman out cold.

From inside, there was the shrill sound of a whistle, and a shout of 'Arrest that man!'

10

Nesting White Tyrants

~ and the loaded gun ~

The journey from Nairobi to the lodge was long, and Bunty was glad finally to be at her home from home in Africa. Shielded from the scorching midday heat and waiting for them on the verandah was Mo – a tall, thin, very upright man in native dress. Mo had lived and worked on the original farmland that now made up the reserve, so knew the place like the back of his hand, and Sidney Brownlee had put Mo in charge of running the estate after the government sold him the land. Alongside Mo was Toto, a scraggy-looking mongrel saur of no description, who was partially blind, lame and missing half its tail. Legend had it that Toto once feared nothing and fought off intruders of every kind, but now it was looked after and loved by all, and was never out of Mo's sight.

'Mrs Brownlee, we are so glad to have you with us.'

Bunty smiled broadly, walked up the steps to join Mo on the verandah, and clasped his hand warmly with both her hands.

'It is so good to be back, Mo!'

Mo's eyes widened as Buster ran in with Carter on his back, and went straight to a water barrel. The tyrant dipped his whole head in with such force that it pushed most of the water out of the sides, drenching Carter, who had leapt off Buster's back and roared with laughter.

'I did say in my letter that we were bringing a surprise,' Bunty said, smiling at Mo. She pointed to the cars parked nearby. 'It looks like we have guests?'

'We almost have a full house,' replied Mo, smiling. Then his smile faded, as he added sadly, 'But I had to turn many people away. They say they want to hunt saurs, not just watch them.'

'Attitudes will change, Mo,' said Bunty confidently. 'And, hopefully, well before all the other safari lodges run out of wildlife.'

'It's still not easy. Hunters are the ones with the money. We may need to think of making some cutbacks,' said Mo. 'When you have rested, we will look at the books. But, for now, we have some paying guests from America.'

'Splendid!' Bunty clapped her hands together. 'Who?'

'An actor I have never heard of and his servants – although he calls them his publicist, agent, stylist and assistant.' Mo looked doubtful. 'None of them seem to do anything.'

'Five rooms, Mo. That is good,' said Bunty.

'And we have one more arriving tomorrow. A photographer, but I don't know when or how he is arriving, as there is no car booked.'

'Gosh, this is exciting!' beamed Bunty. 'Introduce me to everyone, Mo.'

* * *

Theodore stretched after the long journey. It was good to be back. The two allosaurs that Bunty had bought on the train had arrived ahead of them the day before, and been reluctantly reunited with Buster at the stables. After a dust bath, the tyrant had taken refuge in a shaded corner, exhausted from his long run.

Bea had whisked Carter around, familiarising herself again with the place and the old staff, all of whom commented on how she had grown over the last few years. In the kitchen, the cook made some sandwiches and homemade lemonade, which Bea and Carter scoffed down. They were joined by Theodore, who snaffled the last two sandwiches for himself.

'I've just been told by the game warden that some White Titan Tyrants have made their nest close by, and have chicks!' he said, munching.

'How close?' asked Bea eagerly.

'Less than an hour away,' Theodore told her. 'The warden checks them at dusk every day. He's off early today, so I said I'd do it.'

'Did I hear that right?' They turned at the sound of the

American accent, and Bea's mouth dropped open as her eyes fell on the dashing man who stepped into the kitchen. 'Titans close by! Can I tag along?'

Bea blushed deep red, her mouth opening and closing.

'Oh my gosh ... Monty Lomax!' she finally blurted out. She could feel her heart fluttering as she looked into the man's beautiful eyes. *Monty Lomax! The film star! Here!* She was surprised to find he was a lot shorter than she'd expected, but he still had the smile that won over millions of ladies' hearts.

'Thank you, it's nice to be noticed.' Monty smiled and then he gave Bea a wink, which almost made her faint. 'Well ... the White Tyrants, you said something about spotting some close by?'

Monty directed this question at Theodore, who had a good idea who Monty was, and though he'd never seen any of his films, he realised from Bea's reaction that meeting this man was a Big Thing.

'Logan. Theodore Logan,' he introduced himself, shaking Monty's manicured hand. 'Yes. We have room in the car, if you want to tag along?'

'Please do!' burst out Bea, and she blushed again.

'Okay. Let me change and I'll meet you out front.'

With that, Monty started shouting at various people inside to rally around him as he darted off up to his room.

Theodore gave a wider than usual fake smile as he left. 'Brilliant, I'll get the car ready.'

When Monty was out of earshot, Theodore leant into Bea and said: 'Change into what?'

◆ ◆ ◆

It seemed they were waiting for ages in the car for Monty to reappear, but Bea made sure the time was well spent. She filled Theodore and Carter in on all of Monty's greatest movie moments. Carter tried to follow but was instantly lost, and just listened to the sounds of the words. Every now and then he questioned something, to make it look like he was following.

'Bat dark night?'

'No. Battling dark knights in *The Curse of the Round Table*,' Bea explained, as Theodore hooted the horn a third time.

Monty finally appeared from the house. Theodore couldn't resist smiling at the pristine khaki outfit he was wearing; it was straight out of a catalogue. Monty's pith helmet was tilted at the same jaunty angle as his smile, and the sharp creases ironed into his shirt and matching shorts were uncomfortably new.

'Very smart,' Bea complimented him, as Monty trotted over and sat up front with Theodore, placing his rifle between his knees.

'You won't be needing that,' said Theodore. 'We don't hunt saurs here.'

'*You've* got a gun,' Monty pointed out.

'Yes, but I never use it to harm,' said Theodore.

v for protection, in case we run into poachers. We
. ᴜo hunting safaris.'

Monty nodded.

'Understood,' he said. Then he grinned. 'Anyway, this
is only loaded with blanks. It's a prop gun. I can't go on
safari without looking the part!'

Theodore hesitated, then nodded. 'Okay,' he said. 'But
there won't be any shooting. Let's go.'

While Theodore kept alert for any sighting of the
White Tyrants as he drove, Bea kept up a stream of chatter
directed at Monty. Theodore knew she was good at chat,
but this was an hour, non-stop, about all sorts of things
that only she and Monty seemed to understand. Carter
stared out at the landscape, entranced.

Finally, they reached the spot the wardens had told
Theodore to look for. They all quietly walked the short
distance through the shrub, towards a circular clearing.
Theodore motioned to them all to get down and crawl the
rest of the way up to the edge, and there, in plain sight,
was an elegant White Titan Tyrant, crouching next to its
nest hole. Just visible, popping up from within, were some
white feathers, which must have been the chicks.

Carter looked at them, fascinated. He knew this was
another type of tyrant, like Buster, but it was different
in so many ways. The size and colour were the obvious
differences, but he desperately wanted to get a closer look
at the details. The lack of feathers down this tyrant's back,

the thinner and longer neck, its blue eyes and the thinner forearms almost made it seem like a different sort of creature entirely.

'Titans dig out their nests on open territory,' explained Theodore, studying the White Tyrant nest through his binoculars. 'They don't want anything sneaking up on them, so they clear a large circle around them. The chicks are still vulnerable to many other predators – pack animals like hyenas are the worst, as they work together: some distract the adults while the others sneak in to steal the chicks.' He gave a sigh of longing. 'I'd love to be able to get a really close look at it.'

As Theodore handed his binoculars to Bea, he realised Monty was no longer crouched next to him but standing bolt upright and taking aim with his rifle. Quickly, Theodore grabbed the gun from Monty.

'What on earth are you doing?' he demanded. 'I said no shooting!'

'These are blanks!' Monty reminded him defensively.

'The Titan doesn't know that,' said Theodore. 'It hears a shot and the next moment it's over here, very angry, and we'll be its dinner. There is to be no shooting. It could endanger all of us, and we have children here.'

Monty's automatic actor's smile suddenly switched on, and he gave Theodore a wink and a thumbs up.

'Sorry, old pal!' He looked at the White Tyrant again. 'This Titan's a she, right? Where's the male?'

'Off hunting, I expect,' said Theodore. 'He could be close, or miles away. They take it in turns to feed and protect the nest.'

'Might it return soon?' Monty asked.

Theodore nodded.

'That's why we have to be very careful and quiet. It could be sneaking up on us right now.'

At this, Monty gulped nervously and moved into the cover of the car.

Carter looked through his binoculars at the White Tyrant's nest. Theodore had given him his own pair on the boat, and it still amazed him how they magnified everything. Even though he knew the saurs were far away, he couldn't stop himself reaching out to touch them, his brain constantly pulling back on his instincts. A flash of light lit up the lens and attracted his attention towards some bushes past the tyrant.

'Theo!'

Theodore was immediately alert to the note of alarm in Carter's voice.

'What's up, lad?'

'Bad man.'

11

Death on the Battlefield

~ twentieth of April 1917 ~

Theodore looked about intently.

'Where?'

'There.'

Carter kept pointing until Theodore spotted them.

'Looks like two people – no three, possibly more. Hang on, one has a rifle and he's ...' Theodore suddenly swung around to Monty. 'It's poachers. You want to do some shooting?'

Monty seemed wary. His earlier bravado at playing safari had clearly deserted him.

'With blanks?' he said.

'Perfect,' said Theodore, ignoring his reticence. 'If you take up a position over there and shoot over their heads, I'll do the same from here. If we attack from two directions, they'll think there are more of us, and hopefully they'll make a run for it.'

Monty hesitated.

'The thing is, in movies it's usually the stunt men who fire guns, if there's real shooting to be done.'

'We won't actually be shooting at them,' said Theodore.

'But say they shoot at us?' asked Monty, still worried.

Theodore shook his head.

'If they think they're outnumbered, they'll run for it. Trust me.'

Suddenly Monty's worried expression changed to one of firm determination, and, assuming his character, he stood up straight and saluted smartly.

'Leave it to me, general!'

Theodore turned to Bea and Carter. 'You two fall back and get to the car – Bea, start the engine, we may have to leave quickly. Ready, Monty?'

'Sir, yes, sir!' said Monty, and once more he gave a smart salute, before running around to a good position and crouching low, his rifle ready.

Bea looked at Theodore.

'What's all the saluting and that "general" business about?' she asked, bewildered.

'He's an actor,' explained Theodore. 'I've seen it before. They have to take on a different persona to do something properly. Right now, he's a soldier on a mission.'

◆ ◆ ◆

Safely back by the car, Bea and Carter watched through their binoculars as the drama unfolded. The poachers had manoeuvred a bit closer to the nest and were readying their aim, when suddenly Theodore fired, his shot startling them – and the tyrant. It jumped to its feet and began circling the nest at speed. Monty rose from behind his rock and also let off a rain of blank bullets above the poachers' heads, sending them running.

The White Tyrant let out a roar as it spotted the poachers, and gave chase after them, its furious screeching almost drowning out the sound of their car starting up. Theodore aimed towards the engine noise and heard his bullets hit metal. A cloud of dust rose up as the poachers sped away, pursued by the tyrant.

Monty dashed back to the car.

'Where's the general?' he asked Bea, wiping his brow.

Carter gestured urgently at them, still looking through his binoculars, and Bea saw that Theodore's curiosity had got the better of him. He was creeping up to the Titan's nest hole to look inside.

'The general has gone crazy – he's at the nest!' Bea replied.

Just then, a mighty roar shook the ground, and from the rustling trees the mother tyrant burst out and faced Theodore.

'RUN!' shouted Carter.

'Run, Theodore! Run!' Bea joined in.

Theodore ran for his life. The tyrant was making up ground quickly with its powerful long legs bounding the short distance to the nest at the centre of the clearing. Theodore turned to see that the huge Titan was gaining on him – and realised that he was leading the angry saur

towards the children and Monty at the car! He changed direction and stumbled as his legs turned to jelly in fear.

Suddenly Monty jumped into the clearing, raised his rifle, and took aim at the stampeding saur.

'Aim into the air!' Theodore shouted urgently.

'Sir, yes, sir!' Monty replied, and shot above the creature's head. This was enough to startle the enraged tyrant and slow it down.

Theodore and Monty dived back into the cover of the bushes near the car. Losing sight of its quarry, the Titan looked around, then back towards the nest at its chicks. Eventually, with a last roar of warning, she returned to the nest and her mothering duties.

Theodore and Monty were still out of breath when they got back to the car.

'Good work, soldiers!' Theodore looked at Monty with admiration. 'Monty, I've got to say, you showed great courage. You saved my life from the White Titan Tyrant, but you also faced real poachers. And with a gun loaded only with blanks. Soldier, I salute you.'

And with that, Theodore saluted Monty, who snapped to attention and returned it with a smart: 'Just a soldier doing my job, sir!'

✦ ✦ ✦

The drive back was filled with Monty retelling their mini adventure from every camera angle, building up the action and embellishing all the parts they'd each played.

Finally, he said: 'You look to me like the kind of guy who can wrestle a tyrant, Mr Logan. You didn't hesitate out there. I bet you've killed many saurs in your time.'

Theodore hesitated, then said, 'You don't want to hear my stories, Mr Lomax.'

'Sure I do,' said Monty.

'Kill saurs?' repeated Carter, puzzled.

'I've hunted and killed none,' said Theodore firmly. 'I've shot dead many maimed or sick saurs that would have otherwise died slowly in great pain, and I would do it again right now without hesitation if there was no other option.' This statement needed explaining with context to the young ears and to Monty, who knew nothing of Theodore's past.

'Early on in the war, word spread like wildfire that the Hun had a battalion of fearsome berserk saurs. These saurs, mostly European centrosaurs, had somehow been trained to ride into battle against a torrent of gunfire, and devour their enemy. There were only a few horrific cases where they were actually used in battle, but these were enough to put fear into our brave soldiers. You have seen the now famous poster the enemy used to boast about it? Well, it worked. Training saurs to fight humans' battles became fashionable again, and I was drafted in to train allosaurs to ride into the same conditions. But we could never get them to do it of their own free will – you know as well as me, Bea, allos don't like being startled,' Theodore said.

He paused.

'So we needed riders brave enough to face the conditions and lead them into battle, with the aim of riding out alive. Naturally all types of saurs and mammals have been used in warfare for thousands of years, but the last war changed the rule book. Men were pitted against overwhelming odds, horrific conditions, metal tanks, chemical weapons and, now, berserk saurs who feared nothing. Even after being shot they would still limp on and fight, till all their blood was drained.'

'But how did they make them do that?' Bea asked.

'Well, it's still a mystery how they trained them to

do it,' Theodore replied. 'I knew of secret research the Americans conducted using electric shock treatment to try to send saurs crazy, but it was too unstable and inhumane, so it was quickly stopped and we continued with the old-fashioned way of riding saurs, which had not changed since the Roman Empire.'

Monty nodded throughout this explanation. 'So did you see the berserkas? Were those the saurs you killed?'

'No,' Theodore gulped, 'My story is worse ...' He faltered and his voice broke a little. 'I'm responsible for the thousands of allosaurs who died under my charge during the war.'

Everything fell silent. Theodore stared ahead as he drove, and began his story.

'It was the twentieth of April 1917, and I was in northern France. I led a charge over no man's land, towards the enemy, with six squadrons of forty-eight mounted infantrymen. Two hundred and eighty-eight of the finest allosaurs – I'd trained them all myself. After the charge, only twelve returned, riderless but alive. Those allos were so traumatised by what they had gone through that they couldn't be ridden and soon became a liability. It was my job to shoot them a few days later.

'The other two hundred and seventy-six who went over lay where they were cut down by bullets or wire. Most of the riders who were pulled from the killing fields died later from their horrific wounds.'

Theodore paused. The rest of the car was still silent.

'I'll never forget that terrible day,' he went on. 'When night eventually fell, the sound became too much to bear. I couldn't stand to hear the screeches of those wounded saurs any longer. I had no other choice but to walk out into no man's land under cover of darkness, and silence them. I returned with an empty revolver only to refill it over and over again.

'The enemy knew I was there, I came right up to their trenches and looked at them all, the gun in my hand. But I was doing them a service too – the sound of those dying allos was like nothing on earth – so I was spared. Besides, what harm was one lost soul with an empty revolver going to do them?

'I spent all night finishing off what I'd started. I put a bullet in two hundred and seventy-five allosaurs that night, to make sure they were dead, but I couldn't find the last one.

'A week later it was all over. The Allies made advances and the front line was pushed back. A reconnaissance of the enemy's empty trenches found what was left of the last allosaur. It was the only one that had made it to the other side, but it was eaten by the starving troops.'

Overcome with the sadness of his tale, Bea leant forward and hugged Theodore, her tears wetting the back of his head. Carter was not sure why his sister was crying, but from the mood in the car, hugging Theodore felt like the right thing to do, so he joined in.

'Thank you,' Theodore muttered. 'So now you know why I hope I never to have to shoot another saur, Mr Lomax.'

'I'm so sorry, Mr Logan, I had no idea,' said Monty, visibly moved. He, too, wiped away a tear, then added, 'It would make a great movie … *War Saur*.'

12

The Dragonfly

~ *and Micki Myers* ~

Carter was the first to hear the strange noise, and went outside to try to locate it. He shielded his eyes from the sun and looked up towards the buzzing sound. Shaking with excitement, he ran inside to fetch his binoculars.

Bea looked up from her painting kit. 'It's an aeroplane,' she said.

'"Aeroplane"?'

'A car with wings like a bird.'

Carter turned, wide-eyed. Bea smiled back at him as they headed outside.

'Yes, I still think that as well, every time,' she said. 'I still don't understand how it all works. They have big ones, like trains with wings, that carry many people.'

Theodore was outside, looking up at the sky. He lifted his braces on over his shirt.

'Come on – we have a landing strip to clear.'

Theodore backed the Fordson tractor into a shed and coupled it to a large, two-wheeled rake attachment. Bea and Carter jumped on the back of the tractor and they rode to the neighbouring field, where Theodore lowered the rake, and drove backwards and forwards. The rake pulled loose stones all the way out and flattened the grass, leaving a relatively clear path behind it.

With the temporary landing strip ready, Theodore headed back to the lodge with the tractor. As he did, the buzzing noise grew louder and the red biplane swooped down close to the field, low enough for the pilot to wave at Carter, who waved frantically back. The plane looped-the-loop twice, and came in to land.

By now Monty had arrived at the field, with his entourage of assistants. He nudged Bea.

'Now that's an entrance! I must learn to fly one day.'

Bunty also came to see who the visitor was.

'I presume this is the photographer you've all been waiting for?' she enquired of Monty's publicist. 'Mr Myers?'

They all watched as the pilot taxied slowly, killed the engines and jumped out. Wiping bug-splattered goggles, the pilot pulled off a tight leather flying helmet and shook out a long mass of hair.

'Good lord, you're a woman!' exclaimed Monty in amazement.

'Correct – and I was told you're a man, Mr Lomax.' The pilot gave him a grin. 'I hope I'm right. Micki Myers, pleased to meet you.'

As Monty held out his hand to shake hers, Micki slung her jacket onto his arm.

'Thanks. Do be a darling and run a wet cloth over the *Dragonfly*. She's hot, like me, but won't bite as much.'

For once, Monty was dumbstruck.

Bunty stepped forward and shook Micki's hand.

'Welcome,' she said with a smile. 'I'm Barbara Brownlee, but you can call me Bunty.'

'And I'm Beatrice,' Bea introduced herself, 'but friends call me Bea. May I call you Micki?'

Bea held out her hand and Micki gave her a firm handshake.

'Sure, you can call me Micki. Now, you look like a strong girl – come and help me with my equipment and we'll leave the men to look important.'

'Micki, I'd be delighted to carry your bags!' offered Monty, speaking up finally.

'Let's keep it at Miss Myers for now, Mr Lomax,' said Micki. 'Chop-chop now, the *Dragonfly* won't wipe the bugs off herself.'

Monty, in awe and under her spell, darted over to the garage for a bucket.

There was a lot of equipment to be unloaded, but Bea carried the lot over to the house, while Carter stood by the still-vibrating plane, looking at it in awe and wonder.

Theodore came up to Bunty's side.

'Looks like our movie legend has been replaced by a photographer who flies her own plane,' he muttered. 'You're spoiling those kids, Bunty.'

'I wish I could spoil them more,' said Bunty unhappily. 'I had a look at the books yesterday, with Mo. Other lodges charge huge amounts for hunting permits. Meanwhile we're struggling to pay the small number of staff we have here. Let's hope that this photo assignment will be in many magazines around the world, and brings a lot of interest to our lodge. The guest rooms are nearly full at the moment, with Monty Lomax and his entourage and now Miss Myers, but we need to build the reputation of this reserve. So let's make sure things don't mess up, Theo.'

'What would I do to mess things up?' demanded Theodore, slightly offended.

'Yesterday you almost got our film star killed in a crossfire with poachers and a stampeding Titan, for one thing!' she reminded him, her lips pursed in disapproval.

'Oh come on, Bunty,' Theodore defended himself. 'That was hardly my fault. The real problem is that the amazing wildlife we're trying to show people moves across fenceless borders – and so do the vile poachers and big game hunters. It's impossible to have eyes everywhere and keep the saurs safe.'

'True,' admitted Bunty with a sigh. 'But let's do our best to make sure there are no more … adventures.'

+ + +

Bea helped Micki set up a portable photographic studio on the lawn. Over the next few days, Micki planned to shoot portraits of the famous film star Monty Lomax: here, against a white cloth slung between two trees as well as in the wild, at locations that Micki wanted to scout out first.

Having finished wiping the *Dragonfly*, as instructed, Monty tried again to impress Micki. He told her of his heroic battle with the poachers and gave her the full force of his cinematic smile, but she remained resolutely unimpressed as she busied herself with her equipment.

Carter watched Monty following – and being ignored by – Micki, and saw that Monty needed a distraction. So he started to stalk him, in play.

Monty was delighted.

'All righty, let's go on another tyrant hunt!'

The actor crouched into a saur position and let out a roar. Carter laughed with joy. Monty waddled, as if lumbering with a long tail, and pushed his arms back to mimic the tyrant's diminutive forearms, then let out another roar. Carter hissed back, so Monty got even more into the role and bobbed his head, pretending to spot something and sniff.

Carter was thrilled. Until now he had never seen a human mimic a saur. For the first time since leaving Aru, he was able to step back into his old life for a moment. He crouched low and held his usual shadow raptor posture, his head held out forward and his arms back. He tilted his head towards Monty and let out another sinister hiss. Monty roared back and circled him, looking for a weakness ...

At that moment Buster rounded the corner of the lodge, saw what was going on, and dipped his head low – right next to Monty – with a blood-chilling chatter. Monty froze on the spot, then fainted.

Carter burst out laughing, and stroked the tyrant's nose. 'Buster play tyrant!'

♦ ♦ ♦

It took three large brandies and a lot of explaining about Carter's pet tyrant to revive Monty, who was still shaken up an hour later as he left to change for his photo session.

'Monty's a blur of nerves – he'll be no good for a portrait unless he stops trembling,' said Micki, and she suggested that Bunty and Bea posed for their portraits first.

When Monty eventually arrived for his photo session he was wearing another sharply-creased new khaki hunting suit. Unfortunately for Monty, Micki's reaction was laughter.

'You think people go into the bush looking like that?'

she mocked him. She gestured at Theodore, who'd been standing watching the sessions in his crumpled clothes and hat. 'That's what a real man looks like,' said Micki. 'Humble, quiet, knows how to clear a runway – just what every woman needs.'

'You're right,' agreed Monty eagerly. 'That's the man I want to be!'

'Well, start by putting on his clothes,' said Micki.

While Monty and Theodore went off to swap clothes, Bunty asked, 'Would you take a photo of me with my grandchildren?'

Micki smiled. 'It will be my pleasure,' she replied.

Bea ran off to get changed into a smart dress, and grabbed Carter's feathered headdress.

The portrait was stunning, even though it took some time to explain to Carter why he had to stay still. Monty and his stylist were still taking their time so Micki got straight into showing Carter and Bea her portable darkroom and explained the development process as best she could. They followed her every move, as the image appeared on the paper in front of their eyes.

'It's like magic!' breathed Bea in awe.

'I'm so jealous of you,' said Micki enviously.

'Of me?' asked Bea, bewildered.

'Of both of you. I have done things so many times that I struggle to see them with fresh eyes. To you two, everything is new.'

13

An Evening's Entertainment

~ the outdoor cinema ~

That evening, Monty took advantage of Micki's white-cloth backdrop, and proposed a film show. 'We've brought along the first two reels of my latest movie, the one we're here in Africa to get publicity shots for, and a reel or two of my latest blockbuster. We could put some chairs out, rig up a gramophone to play back the sound discs, and we've got ourselves an outdoor cinema. What do you say?'

'I say it's brilliant!' replied Bunty enthusiastically. As the projector and chairs were put in place, she whispered excitedly to Bea, 'Well, this is a first. We should start a movie theatre here!'

Although it took a few attempts to get the sound from the gramophone to sync with the projection, no one minded. To be watching the latest Hollywood movie, alongside its star, beneath the dark African night sky, was a magical experience.

For Carter, the day had already been full of wonders. He was still recovering from the flying car in the sky and the images of himself and his new family appearing on paper, and now he sat stunned that pictures were moving, dancing in light and landing on the white cloth, while their voices lifted from a swirling disc. The movie was called *King Solomon's Mines* and within minutes of it starting Theodore watched Monty shoot at several stunt men with the same gun he'd used on the poachers the day before.

When the first two reels of the movie had been run, Monty stepped up before the makeshift screen and took a bow, to the small audience's applause.

'I'm sure you'll love the whole picture when it's finished.'

Carter clapped the loudest, and this brought Buster over from his stable. His dark silhouette grew large across the white sheet, to everyone's alarm, before he dipped his head under it to see what they were making so much noise about. Monty darted away, but made it look like he only did so to put a reel of another movie, *Robin Hood*, onto the projector.

Carter manoeuvred Buster away, who was just as curious as the boy to see the projection. Bea noticed that Monty rode the same allosaur in this new film, but this time he was at an English castle. The gramophone was unable to catch up and there was a comical lag in the dialogue that seemed to amuse Micki the most.

Monty quickly ended the show before anyone 'else joined in laughing. 'That's all we've got for now, folks.'

'Such a shame we don't have more,' said Bea, who was still mesmerised.

'Well, perhaps you'd like to see my last assignment for *National Geographic*,' suggested Micki.

'Excellent!' said Bunty. 'This is turning into quite an evening's entertainment!'

Micki's slides were stunning, but after the moving images they looked quite static.

'I'm sorry if it doesn't have quite the same showbiz pizzazz, but the story here is about the real mineral mining that's going on here in Africa, not the fictional mines in movies,' said Micki.

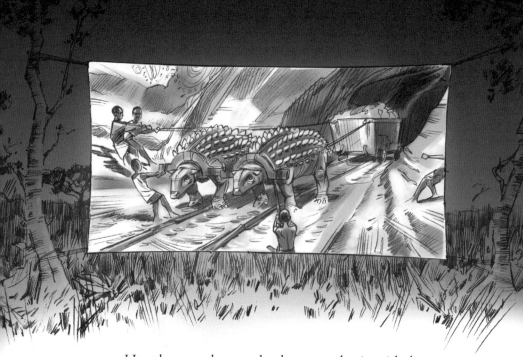

Her photographs were landscapes to begin with, but
soon captured more distressing scenes of open mining in
desolate holes overrun with thin, dirty children.

'Sadly, all this will get ignored. People would rather
wear diamond rings and go to the movies,' said Micki, and
there was no mistaking the anger in her voice.

'Surely it's not all doom and gloom?' protested Bunty.
'There's much more to Africa than this. Especially out
here, in the bush.'

'That may be, but these shots were taken just a few
hours' flight from here,' said Micki.

As more and more harrowing images of desolation
appeared on the screen, and portraits of children and
adults looking starved, and in rags, Micki continued with

her narration: 'These are some of the Steggi tribe. They once roamed all over East Africa, alongside the majestic stegs they coexist with. Now they're turned away from the land, as it is given over to wheat fields, and fenced in. Some are forced to work in the mines in exchange for grazing the stegs on pastures that were once free to them. Others have their stegs stolen or killed by poachers for their bony plates to sell as medicine in the Far East. Soon this way of life will all be gone, just to make a few rich people richer.'

'But how has this been allowed to happen?' burst out Theodore.

'Money and power,' said Micki. 'In these particular pictures, it is because of the very rich man who owns the land next to yours, Mrs Brownlee.'

'Hassler De Bois?' exclaimed Bunty, shocked. 'The diamond merchant?'

'He's much more than a diamond merchant,' said Micki. 'He owns diamond mines. That's his big thing: buying land where diamonds can be found. The man's obsessed with diamonds.' She gestured at the screen. 'It was on his land I took a lot of these pictures, though without him knowing. He's enslaved many of the smaller tribes to work for him, in return for the right to use the land. They thought they were making a deal that would save their way of life, but found they've been tricked into bondage. Slavery. Once, they lived free in this magnificent land, in symbiosis with the majestic saurs. Now they live without hope, and in fear.'

14

Another Boss to Impress

~ such delightful company ~

The next morning, Theodore went out at dawn to saddle the two new allosaurs. Carter was already up, giving Buster a brush. Judging by a small dent in the straw, the boy had made his own nest next to the tyrant and slept there in the stables with him. Both Theodore and Carter were surprised when Bea joined them.

'Take me with you,' she said.

'Where?' asked Theodore. 'I'm just going on a jaunt for a while, perhaps overnight, to break in these two and see what they are made of.'

'No, you're not,' said Bea. 'You're going to visit the Steggi. Please let me come, Theodore. I'll ride the second one with you.'

Theodore looked doubtful.

'It could be dangerous,' he warned her. 'And your grandmother won't let you have any more adventures – she was quite clear. Why not stay here and have some time off?'

'Let's not tell her,' said Bea.

'Beatrice Kingsley,' said Theodore, shaking his head

disapprovingly. 'No more secrets, remember? You need to look after your brother.'

Carter had already figured out that Theodore was about to move off again.

'Me come!' he chirped.

Bea smiled triumphantly.

'Perfect!' she cried. 'I'll look after you both. You go and tell whatever you want to Bunty, Theo, and I'll get my things.'

◆ ◆ ◆

'But why go to the watering hole *now*, of all times?' demanded Bunty, when Theodore told her what he intended to do. 'We have guests who need looking after!'

'*You* have guests, Bunty, and you're better at entertaining them than I am. This will just be a couple of days sleeping under the stars and seeing the wildlife. It'll also keep the children entertained and out of trouble.'

'They aren't any trouble.'

'Carter's tyrant is, and it could do with some retraining. A ride with the new allosaurs will do it good. So will a swim. It might go stir crazy away from water for too long.'

Reluctantly, Bunty nodded. His reasons all added up. Recalling the commotion at the dock, and the incidents on the train and at the polo club still gave Bunty pangs of embarrassment.

'You're right.' But she fixed Theodore with a stare. 'Any sign of trouble, though, and you come straight back here.'

✦ ✦ ✦

Christian Hayter pulled the chauffeur's cap down so the peak shielded his eyes against the sun's dazzle. He hated the cap. He hated the fact that he was wearing a chauffeur's uniform – a servant! But he knew he couldn't afford to be recognised. He'd come face to face with all of them on Aru: that damned Bunty Brownlee, Theodore Logan, Bea Kingsley and the wild boy, Carter. The cap pulled low, with the stiff collar of the jacket partly hiding his face, should do the trick, providing he kept his distance from them. Hayter remembered a story he'd once read, about a waiter who'd committed a murder in a busy restaurant and got away with it, because 'people don't notice servants'.

The road was now marked by bright blue-painted boulders, counting down the miles. BB-10 ... BB-9 ... Nine miles to go. The side roads were simply dirt tracks, but on this more frequently travelled road the traffic had cleared a wider path, confirming – along with the bright blue 'BB' boulders – that this was the road to Bunty Brownlee's lodge. He checked his rear-view mirror to see if his passengers were still asleep, and almost missed the next blue rock: BB-8.

Eight miles to go.

✦ ✦ ✦

'Lambert, how very nice to see you again so soon!'

Bunty skipped down from the verandah with a welcoming smile as Lambert Knútr stepped out of the car.

'It is a joy to be here.' Lambert smiled back at her, and

kissed her hand. 'After you described how wonderful it was, I had to come, and the club became dull without you and the children.'

Bunty linked her arm through Lambert's.

'Come in out of the heat!'

She led her guest to the shady verandah where a tray with cold drinks was soon delivered. She handed a glass to Lambert, who took a long draught and smacked his lips appreciatively.

'That hits the spot!' He smiled.

Bunty looked at the dust-covered car, which was being unloaded by the chauffeur and two other men.

'You must be exhausted after that long drive!'

'Fortunately, I slept most of the way,' said Lambert.

'It was lucky for you that you did,' observed Bunty. 'Your car looks as if it took quite a beating. Did you miss the markers for the main road? It looks as if your driver travelled off-road.'

Lambert gave the briefest of hesitations, then smiled airily as he replied: 'It's funny you should ask. I woke up at one point and it sounded as if someone was shooting at us. I saw we were driving across the bush, so I told the fellow to get back on the road.'

'Oh dear.' Bunty frowned as she saw one of the men dump a case from the car to the ground. 'It can be dangerous out here if you don't know the land. Have they been in your service long?'

'Not long at all,' replied Lambert. 'They came from an agency. My wife can't take the African heat so, at the last minute, she decided to go shopping in Europe and take all our staff. I'd rather she was in safe hands, so those two chaps came on loan, and the driver is from the polo club. I thought it best to use someone who knows the local roads, though perhaps not as well as I'd hoped.' He smiled again. 'Anyhow, we're here now, and with such delightful company.'

Bunty felt herself blushing, surprised at how comfortable she felt with this man.

'The best bit about loaning staff is that you can dismiss them when you don't need them,' continued Lambert. 'If you don't mind, Barbara, I'll let the driver go after he's fixed up the car. Shall I tell him to return in a week? It's ever so kind of you to let me stay and enjoy your company in this beautiful part of the world.'

'Of course you can,' said Bunty, delighted at the idea. 'There are quarters for any of your staff who will be staying. We have some other guests with us, of whom I'm sure you will approve. You may already know of them. Come, let me introduce you.'

◆ ◆ ◆

Christian Hayter was wiping away the dust caked onto the bonnet of the car when a member of Bunty's staff came over with a bucket of water and told him to clean up around the back, out of sight, and not in the main driveway.

Hayter scowled and was on the point of cursing the man when he stopped himself. Being out of sight of everyone suited him just fine. Cleaning the car gave him something to do and blend in. There was no rush, and soon enough some sort of plan would present itself.

He was just finishing a less than professional job when Bishop returned with a pile of sandwiches and some glasses. Ash trotted behind him, holding a jug of fresh lemonade.

'We've been shown our quarters,' said Ash, helping himself to a large, refreshing drink. 'Nice and comfortable, they are.'

'There's a bathtub, and we get to eat three meals a day with the other staff,' added Bishop happily.

'Glad to hear it, I could do with a soak,' said Hayter.

Bishop and Ash exchanged unhappy glances. Then Ash said, awkwardly: 'Uh, sorry, boss. He says he doesn't need a driver any more. You're free to go.'

Hayter stared at them.

'What?' he spat.

'Don't worry, boss,' Bishop added quickly. 'Logan and the kids left this morning, heading east to visit a tribe. If you head off now you could catch them up.'

A nasty smile replaced the scowl on Hayter's face.

'That is good news. Being separated from the pack will make them perfect targets.'

'Will you be okay without my tracking skills, boss?'

Hayter looked both men up and down.

'What skills, you useless fool? It's best you two stick to the plan – keep an eye on things here, and don't do anything stupid. Try to act like proper servants. Don't blow it, do you hear me?' he added menacingly. 'You have another boss to impress while I'm away.'

15

The Watering Hole

~ the killing field ~

Bea woke to the sound of water splashing. The previous evening they'd brought Buster and the two allosaurs to a halt as night fell, and tethered them to a tree near a watering hole. Bea had begun to help Theodore and Carter put up the tent, but then a casual glance up at the sky had claimed her full attention while they finished the job. The stars! She'd never seen so many!

At sea, they'd always been below decks before dusk, and since they'd arrived on land everything had been so busy, busy, busy. But here, in the vastness of the landscape, with the bush spreading out away from them, the sky was ... endless, a galaxy of stars. She'd sat down on the ground and let herself be absorbed by the immenseness of the night sky, and only became dimly aware of Theodore and Carter when they sat down beside her, their eyes, too, taking in the wonder above.

The gathering cool of the night eventually forced them into the tent, with Bea dropping into a deep sleep – until the sounds of splashing water filtered through to her brain.

She sat up. Carter was gone.

'Theodore,' she called gently.

Theodore opened his eyes, then sat up, pushing his blanket away and following Bea as she pushed her way through the tent flap.

Outside, dawn had broken, and both stood open-mouthed in awe at the glorious spectacle in front of them.

The watering hole was alive with light, every drop of moisture sparkling, like millions of diamonds. Bathing in the centre of the pool was Carter, joyfully splashing water up into the air in arcs that flared out iridescent flashes of rainbow. An Appato of huge proportions swooped its head low and lifted a plume of water over Carter in a shower of sparkles that seemed to fall slowly, and hit the surface like glass shattering. Four or five elephants, dwarfed in comparison, were spurting water from their trunks in the shimmering shallows. Surrounding them, rheboks danced as a herd of Thinhorn Tritops gently wallowed deeper in, lifting their heads, their brow horns almost pointed to the sky. A host of Sidespines thwacked their spiny tails into the water, which scared the few, brave red-leg pretors into the air, to resettle further away, safely next to a variety of storks.

'It's magical!' breathed Bea.

♦ ♦ ♦

Once they were on the move, after a light breakfast, the three riders took turns in the lead. As Bea led the way on her allosaur, she looked out at the vast terrain stretching out before them and noticed the parched dryness of the veld with its coarse brambles, termite mounds and long grass that any predator could use to hide.

Buster and Carter seemed to pick up a whiff of something, and broke into a trot, overtaking Bea's allosaur, whose nostrils flared as it sought the scent. Theodore drew alongside Bea and looked at Carter with pride.

'He's amazing,' he said. 'How quickly he's picked up riding that tyrant bareback – which isn't easy, even on a well-trained allosaur. Look at the way he grips slightly between his thighs on every forward step, relaxing on the second, rocking himself in the same rhythm as the beast as if he was part of it.'

Theodore had ridden enough allosaurs bareback in his youth – on the Kingsley ranch back in America with Franklin and Cash – to know what he was talking about. 'It's special when you bond with a saur. It's like you're one and the same animal, moving to the same beat. Your father was the best rider I ever knew, Bea. He knew how riding bareback, the way Carter does, not only makes it smoother for the rider, but massages the saur's back at the same time, eliminating the muscle cramp that a saddle causes. It means the saur can go for longer distances, and enjoy it rather than endure it.' He glanced at his goddaughter. 'And you're another one with Kingsley's talent, Bea. Look at how well you ride!'

Yes, thought Bea. She did find it easy to ride, more so than all her friends at school. Was it because Theodore had trained her well, or did she really have her father's way with saurs?

'Nature or nurture?' she blurted out loud, half as a statement and half as a question.

'Nature *and* nurture, in my book,' said Theodore. 'That boy also has a lot to learn which you already know. He would have no idea that blackberries make allosaurs sick, or that chewing mint after meat helps their poo smell better.'

Bea nodded. Nature and nurture. Theodore was always right.

Suddenly the allosaurs picked up the scent that the tyrant had caught five minutes earlier. Both saurs lowered their heads, filled their nostrils like hunting dogs, and picked up the pace.

The pathway went up a ridge, over which Carter had already disappeared on Buster. As Bea and Theodore drew atop the ridge, both looked at each other with concern. The smell of death was well known to them. The smell of rotting flesh is unmistakable, and here it was overpowering. A dead saur lay on the ground, a dark cloud of flies above it.

'Judging by the thin, blade-like plates along its spine, it's a young kruger,' said Theodore. 'Probably got separated from the herd and killed, but it's strange that it's whole and not half eaten.'

'What do you mean?'

'Allosaurs, tyrants, lions, hyenas – practically all meat-eating predators have an amazing sense of smell. Scavenging takes a lot less energy than hunting,' Theodore reminded her. 'The slightest hint of meat decay can be pinpointed to a source that can sometimes be hundreds of miles away. The challenge is to be one of the first to exploit the free meal. The bigger and meaner you are, the more likely you will eat first, or scare off something else that's got there before you.'

Carter had already dismounted his Black Tyrant and was sitting in the shade under a curiously wide tree, while Buster fed on the dead kruger's flesh. Theodore dismounted from his allosaur and let it trot over to join the tyrant.

'Best take this opportunity and let the allosaurs feed, Bea. We can rest for a while here, upwind of the smell.'

As they strode up to the tree to join Carter, Theodore slipped on some loose soil and tumbled into a shallow hole.

'That's strange,' he said, clambering out of the hole and dusting himself down. 'This has only recently been dug.'

Bea lifted a crude shovel out of a bush next to the hole.

'Maybe someone was going to bury the kruger?' she said.

She tossed the shovel into the hole and stood still, her nose wrinkled.

'That's a very bad smell for just one dead saur,' she said. 'It must have been lying here for days, but it doesn't look like it has.'

She took a swig from her water caddy and passed it to Carter, who silently sipped, then spoke.

'Smell bad bad. And listen noise.'

'Yes,' agreed Theodore, nodding. 'It's the buzzing of flies, but it's too loud to be coming from just that dead saur.'

He saw that Buster had abandoned the carcass, and had disappeared over another ridge.

'Something's not right,' he muttered.

Theodore left the shade of the tree, followed the tyrant's tracks to the crest of the ridge, and suddenly stopped.

'Oh my lord!'

Bea and Carter heard the shock in his voice, and hurried to join him. It took a moment for the full horror of what lay before them to sink in. Dead krugers lay scattered as far as the eye could see. Buster was already feeding, as were the millions of flies, and a threat of bald pterosaurs were descending from the sky.

Theodore went over to investigate the nearest carcass, pinching his nose to block out the smell. Carter followed him.

Bea watched them in silence. Theodore was examining the ground, turning things over with the toe of his boot, while Carter was studying the dead krugers in close detail. *Something's missing*, thought Bea as she watched. And then she realised. All of the kruger's bony plates were gone.

Carter called Theodore over. He was near the largest carcass now. Carter walked up the length of the body, from the tail, and began jumping up and down on its ribcage. Theodore gestured for him to keep doing it as he examined the body.

'Yep, you're right.' He nodded. 'Body fluids seeping out.'

The two of them tried to lift the dead kruger's legs up and rock it onto its curved back, but the dead weight defeated them.

'Looks like the first one we found ran off when it was wounded and collapsed over there, away from the rest of the herd,' said Theodore. 'It was spared the indignity the others faced. They've been shot and their plates removed. Hacked off where they lay.'

'Why were you looking at the big one?' asked Bea.

'Its head has been cut off. And after its blades were

removed it must have been rolled onto its back, and something was removed from its belly.'

'That's horrid!' said Bea, shuddering.

'It's horrid and strange,' said Theodore thoughtfully. 'It would have taken a few men to do it.'

'Could it have been the hunters we spotted?' Bea suggested.

'Maybe. The head removal was from the alpha male, so that it looks like a trophy kill, but it's more likely poachers were filling an overseas order for plates. A big order,' he said grimly. He pointed at the ground. 'There are tyre tracks here, so they came equipped.'

'But why?' Bea asked.

'Money. It's always about money.'

'Always money,' echoed a voice behind them.

16

The Stegosorcerer

~ *the Ronax* ~

The figure who stepped from behind the tree was tall and thin. He wore a bright crimson cloth wrapped around him and was covered in loops of small colourful beads. He was holding a long staff with four small stegosaur tail spikes on one end. In complete contrast to this traditional dress he also wore a white bow tie and a wristwatch, bunched up between the bands of fine beads that ran halfway up his arm. Bea was relieved to see he was smiling at them in a kindly manner.

'How long have you been there?' Bea asked.

'I've been waiting for you a *long* time.' He emphasised the word 'long'.

'Who are you?' asked Theodore.

'I have many names and many lives, but now call me Stegosorcerer.'

'You're from the Steggi tribe?' Bea asked.

'That is partly truth, yes.'

'Great.' Theodore smiled. 'I'm Theodore Logan, and

this is Bea, and Carter. We were trekking to visit the Steggi. Can you show us the way?'

'Yes.' The man nodded. 'I've come to collect you. We meet under the sacred tree.'

Theodore looked at the field of dead krugers.

'Do you know what happened here?'

'It is very sad, and must end,' the man said. 'I have a message, but for whom?'

Theodore struggled to understand what the man meant.

'Yes, *I* have an important message for you and the Steggi,' Theodore told the man.

'Theodore, I think we ought to leave this message stuff till later,' said Bea, worried. 'If our allosaurs and the vultures have smelled lunch, won't other carnivornes come too?'

Some vultures had arrived and were squabbling with Buster, the allosaurs and the bald pteros, regardless of the fact there was plenty to go around.

Bea climbed the strange tree to get a good view, and scanned the area. In a patch of open grass she saw what she feared, making a pathway towards them.

'Ronax Tyrants heading this way!' she shouted. 'A pack of them, and coming fast!'

She clambered back down.

'Right, let's get out of here!' said Theodore. He turned to the stegosorcerer. 'Which way do we go?'

The stegosorcerer ignored him and ran over to the shallow hole Theodore had fallen into, picked up his shovel and began digging.

'What are you doing?' asked Theodore, bewildered.

'Must finish digging my hole,' the skinny man screeched back. 'It has to catch a bad man.'

Theodore stared at him in frustration.

'That hole won't catch anything! It needs to be a lot deeper and hidden.'

'*You* fell in,' the stegosorcerer retorted.

'The Ronax!' whispered Bea urgently.

The allosaurs had suddenly become aware of the fast-approaching tyrants, and as the first Ronax appeared both of them bolted in panic.

'Damn! We should have tied them!' said Theodore, angry at himself.

Carter stood in awe at how well the Ronax blended in. It had been hard to spot them against the scrubland and grass, but he was used to seeing invisible shadows. Like tigers, they had stripes to diffuse their outline, but these were of rust red, beige and tan. Their heads were long and pointed, not blunt like Buster's or the Titan's.

Fortunately, the first Ronax hadn't noticed them yet. It had headed straight for a dead kruger, sinking its head in for a bite of the soft innards, which the allos had exposed.

'Come on, let's get out of here! We don't have much time!' urged Theodore.

He grabbed the stegosorcerer by the arm to hustle him away, but he appeared rooted to the spot, and was still clutching his spade.

Bea and Carter ducked out from under the low branches of the tree, just as another Ronax appeared in front of them all.

Theodore let go of the stegosorcerer as Carter pushed his way in front of the Ronax. Bea noticed the Ronax tilted and tipped its head left and right, exactly the same way shadow raptors did. Carter noted this too, and did the same back.

'This close up it loses sight of what's directly in front of it, and has to compensate for its blind spot,' said Theodore. 'Stay very still, and it might not see us.'

The Ronax let out a short, high-pitched bark, like the yap of a small dog.

Carter barked back instantly.

Theodore groaned at the sound. The Ronax tilted its head more to the left and stared from just one eye.

Suddenly there were more yapping sounds from all around them.

Bea spun around but could not see the predators: they were too well hidden in the bushes and long grass.

Carter yapped again, but this time the reply was very different. Not yapping, but a deep roar. Buster had appeared beside them.

The Ronax cautiously stepped back.

The stegosorcerer tapped Theodore's arm. 'We run.'

'No!' said Theodore, grabbing his arm and holding on. 'No one move. They want to single us out.'

Buster had never seen a Ronax before, and looked at it with curiosity. This Ronax had obviously never seen a Black Tyrant either, and, with the confidence of the pack behind it, was just as curious to size up the new enemy.

Buster reprised his chatter at a deeper tone and drooled, before letting out a long low roar to state his intentions.

Another Ronax stepped forward. This Ronax was even larger, probably the alpha male. It began to circle them. In response, Buster let out a rattling chatter with another long growl, which intensified the situation.

'There's no way Buster can deal with all these Ronax,' muttered Theodore.

'But Buster was the top predator where he came from, until Hayter captured him,' Bea said.

'Yes,' agreed Theodore quietly. 'But it also means he's not used to other saurs being a match for him. And since he's been free, he hasn't needed to worry about any of this. Until now.'

Carter had remained silent in front of the tyrant. His bark hadn't been to try to make friends but to get the others to bark back. Being brought up by a clan of shadow raptors had taught him all the ways to hide, to blend in and not to be seen. The Ronax had grass rather than trees to hide in, but their methods were the same. Their return barks had given them away, as did their slow breathing and the dust underfoot, as they edged closer.

All of this had confirmed what Carter had initially feared: they were surrounded, and seriously outnumbered. Making friends was not going to pull them out of this predicament.

The boy and his saur looked at each other. Buster had come to the same conclusion.

Carter raised a hand and patted his dear friend. It was time for them to say goodbye.

Buster rubbed the side of his head into Carter and snorted, and Carter snorted back.

'Go!' said Carter, and he slapped Buster, who bolted off at speed.

Immediately, the Ronax pack gave chase after the tyrant, shrieking and barking.

Carter watched Buster run off into the long grass, with the Ronax in hot pursuit.

'We go!' he said, and together they ran off in the opposite direction.

When they were a good distance away, Carter stopped and turned. Now all he could see were clouds of dust as the Ronax and Buster disappeared from view. Tears sprang into his eyes. Bea put a sisterly arm around his shoulder. She was unsure at first why Buster had run off but had concluded that it was the only way for them to get out alive and the magnificent tyrant somehow knew this.

Carter lifted a hand and whispered, 'Friend.'

17

The Steggi

~ the stegs ~

The stegosorcerer led them on a route that used barely visible paths over the rough terrain. Without the allosaurs, it was tough-going. Bea noticed that Carter, barefoot as he preferred – like the stegosorcerer – was finding it a lot easier than she and Theodore. She pointed to Carter's feet and asked Theodore: 'Should I also … ?'

Theodore shook his head.

'No. Your soft skin won't last a few yards on this terrain. Thorns, barbs, brambles, spikes, splinters; and they're just the things that won't bite, sting, scratch or burrow.'

'How can Carter manage then?' Bea said, bewildered.

'He's had eleven years of being barefoot; his feet have become harder.'

'Not like yours, then?' Bea smiled, gesturing at Theodore's big heavy boots.

Theodore gave a painful grimace.

'My feet are a different story. I never take off my boots, if I can avoid it.'

Something in his tone made Bea look at him inquisitively. 'Is this another of your sad war stories?'

'This one is much more gruesome,' Theodore said seriously. Then he forced a grin. 'But don't worry, I'll save it for when you're really happy.'

It wasn't long before they spotted their first herd of stegs on the horizon, the unmistakable bony plates fanned out across their backs and shimmering in the heat haze. As they grew closer to the herd, they came to some flat and lush pastures where the stegs grazed – and what looked like a village in the distance, with a few trails of smoke rising into the late-afternoon sun. The stegs, curious about these new arrivals, headed towards them.

'My, these stegs are twice the size of the krugers and krynos,' said Bea, as the stegs gathered around them.

'Be careful,' warned Theodore. 'If a herd gets too close and too curious, they can accidentally crush you.'

The huge creatures' heads, tiny in comparison to their bodies, hung down at roughly waist height and would occasionally swing towards the humans to take a sniff. Their beak-like mouths constantly chewed the cud, like cows. Bea patted one on the head, which it seemed to like. As it passed, she ran her hand along its side and noticed a strange patterning on its back and plates. She looked at the rest and exclaimed: 'They've all got handprints on them!'

'That is interesting.' Theodore came in close to one and held out his large hand over one of the prints. 'It looks like they're all children's handprints. I'm guessing the mud layer acts as a sun block.'

'And identification,' added a small voice from somewhere above them.

Startled, they looked up. A shaven-headed boy was sitting on the steg, between the top two bony plates. He was covered in the same pale markings as the steg, and it took a moment for them to pick him out.

'Hello up there. I'm Bea!' she called.

'Hullu.' The boy smiled down at them. 'I'm Sholo, and only my stegs have my handprints.' As he spoke he opened his hand to show them his white palm.

'Well, that's clever,' said Theodore admiringly.

'And it's not mud,' the boy added.

'Oh? What is it then?' asked Bea.

'Ash clay.'

He reached down and lowered his hand for Bea to rub her thumb over. A thin layer of white dust lifted off onto her thumb.

'Amazing!'

The boy smiled. 'You want to ride up here?'

'Yes please!' said Bea.

She reached up, grabbed the steg's bony plates, then Theodore gave her a boost as she clambered up the creature to join the boy in his position high up on the steg's shoulders. She looked at the rest of the herd and noticed that atop many of the other stegs were other children, who all gave her a wave. A few stegs away, Carter was also climbing up, and he waved at his sister excitedly.

'Room for me up there?' Theodore shouted.

'Sorry, no big men,' replied Sholo. 'Only little men and women.'

Bea looked around. There were no adults riding.

'Why no big men?'

'Stegs belong to children,' said Sholo. 'We look after them.'

'But what happens when you grow up?'

'Mine will pass to my younger brothers or cousins when I am too old. Then I will become a civil engineer or a train driver.'

It was such an unexpected thing to hear, out in the bush, that Bea laughed happily. I am going to enjoy getting to know the Steggi tribe, she thought to herself.

The children turned their stegs to follow the stegosorcerer as he headed for the village with Theodore. Three tall elderly men, adorned with a myriad of colourful beads hanging over the crimson cloths tied around their waists, were waiting for them. Behind the elders, all the other adults had gathered, not dressed as spectacularly, but with fantastically coloured beads looped all over them.

'Hullu. You have finally come. The stegosorcerer told us to be expecting you,' the oldest said, smiling at them.

Theodore stepped forward and shook the man's hand.

'I'm Theodore Logan, and these are Beatrice and Carter Kingsley.'

Bea and Carter dismounted from their stegs and bowed to the elders.

'They are your children?'

'No, I am their guardian, who protects them,' answered Theodore.

'Your guardian has done well to bring you here,' said an elder to Bea and Carter. 'Welcome to the Steggi.'

'I apologise for this intrusion,' continued Theodore. 'I have come with a request. We are in need of your help and would like to repay you with terms we hope you will find favourable. I'm sure you'll like what we have to offer.'

The three men looked at each other, puzzled.

'But this is not why the sorcerer said you would come.'

Theodore looked at the stegosorcerer, confused. Had he predicted their arrival here? How?

The three men leant towards one another and mumbled very quietly together, then the oldest-looking announced: 'We do not like this word "offer", but we have already prepared a feast in your honour. Please, stay for the night, and we will find the time to talk with you. Come.'

The elders led Theodore and the two children to a circle of huts surrounding a large fire. As they walked, Bea whispered to Theodore: 'But how did they know we were coming?'

'Something strange is going on here,' Theodore whispered back. 'Whatever it is, I don't think we've lived up to the stegosorcerer's description. When I mentioned an offer it felt like suddenly we lost their trust. We need to win them over – so lots of smiles, please.'

'This will be yours for the night,' said the elder, as they reached an empty hut with woven mats on the floor.

Theodore looked at the hut, impressed. It was made of flat panels of dried grass that were woven together inside a frame, with longer panels for the roof.

'This is genius,' he said. 'These can be simply dismantled and packed flat when they move to a new location.'

Sholo appeared beside them and tapped Bea and Carter on the arm. 'Children stay with the stegs,' he said. 'Come, join us.'

Theodore nodded.

'Good idea,' he whispered. 'If you win over the kids, maybe I'll win over the elders.'

Outside the circle of huts, the stegs were gathered around large mounds, calling out to each other with echoing honks. As they got closer, Bea saw that the mounds were built from dried layers of steg-dung pats, and were being lit from embers brought from the communal fire.

Carter and Bea sat down and watched Sholo and his friend blow the smouldering embers alight. Then Sholo stood up and called out 'Sheia! Sheia!'

An older girl – her hair tightly braided, and wearing a long, patterned length of fabric that was tied up over one shoulder – joined them. Like the rest of the tribe she was very tall.

'Hullu!' She smiled. 'I'm Sheia.'

'I'm Bea.' Bea smiled back.

'My sister has beads for you,' said Sholo.

Sheia took a line of beads from the magnificent array around her waist and placed them over Bea's head.

'Thank you,' said Bea. 'They are beautiful.'

Carter touched the delicate balls of colour and ran his fingers over them. Sheia saw this and giggled, then removed a bracelet from her wrist and handed it to him.

'I'm Carter,' he smiled. 'Hullu.'

Sholo smiled. 'You're both quick to learn!'

'Come, meet my friends!' said Sheia, and she took Bea by the hand and whisked her away to join the other girls.

Meanwhile, Carter was watching the fire grow and the stegs settling down around it. The smoke grew thicker and the stegs' honking lowered a tone as they sat down. Sholo took a few handfuls of dry ash from the previous fire and dusted himself down with it, making sure it was well rubbed into his closely cropped hair. Carter unbuttoned his shirt and stuffed it into his satchel, then picked up a handful of ash and put it on himself. The first handful stuck to his hot sweaty body, forming a crust which the second and third handfuls clung to. As Carter smeared more ash on himself, it cooled his body down and he stopped sweating. Sholo helped him rub it over his back, where it was harder to reach, and onto his stubbly scalp. They both smiled and held out their arms. Both boys were now the same colour.

Carter breathed in deeply, then let out a perfect long and low steg honk, which resounded around the herd, and produced honking replies from all of them.

'Wow!' said Sholo, impressed.

* * *

Theodore wandered over and sat with the stegosorcerer and the three tribal elders outside what looked to be the main hut. The one who did the talking was called simply 'the Elder', in the same way everyone called the strange man in a bow tie the stegosorcerer.

'I have travelled two days from the west to offer you free grazing and movement on land my friend owns,' said Theodore. 'In return we ask that you watch over it and inform us if you see poachers or hunters crossing into it. We have many White Titan Tyrants we want to protect from being killed for sport.'

The Elder considered this, then said carefully: 'We have moved around these lands for thousands of years. Then people like you come and try to change our beliefs, teach us your words and tell us there are lines in the earth that we cannot step beyond.' He shook his head. 'Our stegs will be hunted like your Titans, and our spears are no match for poacher's bullets. We cannot be of any help to you.'

'We are not like the people you have met before,' Theodore insisted. 'My friend wishes to protect your stegs from harm.'

'How can we trust you?' asked the Elder. 'Another man offered us free passage on this land, in return for help finding minerals that are hidden in the ground. We declined, and now he still demands we work for him. What makes you different from him?'

'The land my friend owns was part of the old farming community run by Mo Dengwa,' explained Theodore. 'When the government wanted to sell the land and move him away, my friend stopped this. Mo still manages the land, like his family before him, and we are protecting it for future generations. The world is changing, and I agree it is not necessarily for the good, but if we work together I am sure we can help each other.'

The mention of Mo's name seemed to interest them. The Elder turned to the two other, and they conversed in low tones.

Finally, the Elder turned back to Logan and told him: 'After the feast and dancing, boys from our tribe will become men, and prove themselves by walking over the fire. If you want us to trust you, then you must prove your words are true. Logan, you will also walk over the hot fire.'

18

Feast and Fire

~ a very special occasion ~

Later that evening, after the feasting, the round fire was flattened out into a long blanket of burning-hot embers that glowed as the evening breeze swept over it. A group of the older boys stood up and paraded around, mentally preparing themselves, and giving each other confidence for the task ahead. To psych themselves up they started to chant, and the whole tribe joined in.

Carter and Bea sidled up behind Theodore.

'Is it true?' Bea questioned him worriedly. 'Are you also going to walk on the fire?'

'I have to,' said Theodore. 'They need to know we can be trusted.'

'But you'll be burned, Theodore!' Bea looked tearful at the thought. 'You said yourself you wouldn't walk barefoot – and this is worse!'

Carter leant in. 'I do it,' he said. And he pointed at his dirty bare feet.

'No you will not!' said Bea firmly. 'Neither of you should. Oh, Theodore, please don't!'

Theodore turned and looked at them both.

'*You* have to trust me on this, like *they* need to trust me. I'll be fine.'

The Elder stood up and made an announcement, and a hush fell over the gathering. The moment had come. The stegosorcerer stepped forward to the fire and waved his staff over the glowing embers, then sprinkled some kind of dust on them that made the coals glow even more brightly. He made a last declamation and stepped back.

The first Steggi youth lined himself up at the start, squared his shoulders, kept his eyes focused on the other side, and started to pace on the spot. The crowd began to chant, urging him to walk.

The waiting was painful for Bea, who could not bear to watch but equally did not dare to turn away. Carter looked on intently as the embers crackled and popped.

Suddenly the Steggi youth moved forward and paced across the fire, chanting along with the tribe.

The crowd erupted and took to their feet, jumping for joy when he finally reached the end.

For the second Steggi, the chanting went up a notch. Unlike the first, he was not hanging about. He went straight onto the fire and paced in time to the chanting, all the way to the end. He leapt for joy on his last step, and landed on the cold ground with a sizzle.

It was obvious to all that the third Steggi boy's faith was waning, because he was visibly shaking. He hesitated by the beginning of the fire trail, then did a very foolish thing – dipping a toe into the hot embers to test the heat – and everyone saw him wince and recoil in pain.

The decision was taken from him when the fourth Steggi lost patience and pushed him on. No one seemed to mind that the boy immediately broke into a run; everyone was just pleased to see another young man cross the hot embers and reach the end.

Bea could feel the boy's pain, and her anxiety for Theodore increased.

The next two Steggi both made it in good time, at more of a very quick pace than a walk, but the crowd was flagging and the chanting seemed to have lost its energy.

The last boy was by far the shortest, although in a tribe of tall people like the Steggi, that meant he was still as tall at Theodore. The boy wavered, then turned away from the fire, his head hung low with shame, and walked away.

The stegosorcerer saw this and shouted to the tribe to give this last boy everything they had in support. The tribe responded, and clapped, stamped and chanted louder than they had before. Louder and louder grew the chanting and the clapping and the stamping, urging the boy back.

The boy, who was nearly beyond the light from the fire, stopped, then turned. As the chanting and clapping grew still louder, he seemed to grow taller. He marched back to the firepit, then walked across the glowing embers. With each step he seemed to grow even taller, and when he came to the end he gave a shout of joy.

The three elders stood and the tribe fell into silence. The oldest raised his arms and addressed the tribe in their native tongue for some time, before turning and facing Theodore.

'Now it is your time. You need to win the heart of the tribe for us to follow you. If you can't take the heat, then turn around and walk away for ever!'

Theodore nodded. He turned to Bea and muttered: 'I said I'd never take these boots off, except for a very special occasion. I guess this qualifies.'

He unlaced his boots and took them, and his socks, off, then walked barefoot to the end of the firepit.

Bea shook her head, worried. Carter watched, wide-eyed. Theodore looked around at the whole Steggi tribe, who were watching him in silent expectation.

'How about a bit of chanting, or a clap or two?' Theodore appealed.

Sholo stood bolt upright and started a mighty hand clap. Sheia, next to him, joined in. Carter and Bea stood together and made it louder, before the rest started to applaud and whistle. The stegosorcerer started a chant, then he sprinkled more of his secret dust onto the embers, reigniting them and sending snap, crackle and pops of red-hot sparks high into the air.

'Great,' Theodore muttered. 'Even hotter for the new kid, why not?'

He looked towards Carter and Bea, who mouthed 'Don't do it!' very obviously to him; then he turned his attention to the far end of the fire.

Theodore slowly raised his left foot and placed it firmly onto the glowing embers that sparked up around it. Then, rather than quickly stepping on with his right foot, he dug his left foot in deeper until it sank into the hot coals. He glanced down, shrugged, and calmly proceeded to walk forward one step at a time, as if it was a pleasurable afternoon on the beach. The tribe fell silent. Even Carter stopped mid-clap with shock. The Elder was so astonished his long pipe fell from his open mouth, to the ground.

Theodore saw that he had the whole tribe's full attention now. He stopped halfway along the path of the fire, took a step to the side and picked up the Elder's pipe off the floor where it had toppled. Seeing that it had gone out, Theodore used the bowl of the pipe to scoop up a burning hot coal, and proceeded to relight it. He passed it back to the Elder with a smile.

'Nasty habit that. Suggest you give it up, old boy,' he remarked.

The Elder took the pipe and stared at Theodore in utter disbelief. The whole tribe was transfixed.

Theodore was still standing on the fire – he had been there for much longer than all the others put together and he was still only halfway across. He leisurely walked to the end with a joyful whistle. But before he stepped off, he wiped his feet on the last of the hot coals as if it was a doormat. He rejoined the open-mouthed Bea and Carter.

'Theo, how did you do that?' Bea demanded. 'Why aren't you hurt?'

'It's a long and gruesome story,' muttered Theodore, looking ruefully at his feet, which were still smouldering and blackened. 'I'll tell you another time.'

'Oh please, Theodore! You could shorten it – and remove the gory and nasty bits?'

Theodore breathed in deeply.

'North Atlantic, dead of night: we were rocked by a torpedo and our gunship took on water fast. It was dark and we had no time to do anything, not even to put on our boots. I was on deck for no more than two or three minutes waiting to get in the lifeboat, but it was too long.' He grimaced. 'My feet froze to the metal deck.'

Theodore lifted a foot and dusted off some burning embers that were still embedded there, showing Bea his flat and creaseless sole.

'Luckily, the only soles that went down with the gunship were mine. I had to be pulled into the lifeboat screaming. We got to shore and were helped by an

Icelandic family. Days later I awoke with my raw feet hanging off the bed, being licked clean by their pet wimersaur. Apparently it's and old local trick, and they healed beyond anyone's expectations, but to this day I can't feel a thing.'

Bea squirmed at this story, but shook it off and hugged him again. She kissed him on the cheek, bursting with pride, while Sholo and Sheia led the tribe, as they clapped and stamped and cheered.

19

Herding the Stegs

~ overdue rent ~

Dawn started early. The smouldering dung fires had burned down, and thin wafts of white smoke lifted from them gently. Sholo pulled the last of the embers to one side of the mound of ash, and re-stoked it with some more dried dung. He puffed away till it was glowing again. Carter, tucked up next to a snoring

steg, rubbed his eyes open as someone came by with a bucket of water. Sholo took a cupful and poured it onto the pile of warm ash. With a stick, he started to mix it up into a smooth paste.

'Ash clay. Come, you help me pat down my stegs.'

Sunlight had warmed the stegs awake. With a snort and a grunt they slowly made their way up onto all four feet. The plates along their spines had a surprising amount of movement, and flapped as they all shook out the night.

The stegs stood patiently around the newly lit fire, bathed in the drifting smoke that hung close to the ground. Carter watched Sholo slap his handprints along the side of the first steg before he began decorating one himself.

Bea made her way over.

'Morning. The girls and I have made breakfast. I'm not sure what the steg egg is mixed with but it tastes pretty good.'

'First paint,' said Carter.

'Okay with me.' Bea nodded. 'I've seen Theodore, he wants to help pack up the tribe's huts, and says we can go on ahead with Sholo and Sheia.'

The Steggi children took the role of herding the stegs very seriously. It was a responsibility at the heart of their tribe, and was bestowed upon them with huge amounts of trust. All the children had their own jobs: young girls collected eggs and helped incubate them in woven baskets of straw. The youngest Steggi decorated the infant stegs with the smallest of handprints while these small saurs – with more rounded plates – rolled about in the ash. And the young human boys ran about playing chase with the more energetic stegs.

When Carter and Sholo eventually came over for breakfast, Carter had a fresh layer of ash entirely covering him and, with his shaven head, if it hadn't been for his cold blue eyes, he was almost indistinguishable from the other boys in the tribe.

'He just becomes invisible,' said Theodore admiringly. 'Like when he was with the shadow raptors.' He looked at Bea and nodded. 'You've blended in well, too,' he said.

Bea looked down at the colourful tribal dress she wore, which was adorned with beautiful beads.

'I do like this look,' she said. 'I thought the colour wouldn't go with my complexion, but I think it does!'

Theodore laughed. 'Fashion sense!' he chuckled. 'Even out here in the bush.'

It took a few hours for all the children and their stegs to get ready and head off, in waves of migration. Loading the huts and belongings onto the larger stegs, securing them firmly to make sure nothing fell off on the journey, took longer and was a job for the adults. Theodore and

the stegosorcerer were inside the last of the huts, about to take it apart, when Theodore heard the thudding feet of an allosaur. Curious, he was on the point of stepping outside to see who had arrived when the stegosorcerer grabbed him and held him back, signalling for him to stay inside the hut and be silent.

Theodore nodded and found a gap between two panels to peer out through, while the stegosorcerer went to greet the new arrival.

Theodore recognised the visitor: Hassler De Bois!

The diamond merchant pulled to a halt by the stegosorcerer and the three village elders.

De Bois surveyed the almost completely dismantled village and said: 'Going somewhere? I do hope you have accepted my offer. I would remind you that it's been six months now, and I have been very patient.'

'We cannot work for you, sir,' replied the Elder politely. 'Sadly, it is time for us to leave this land that you have made a claim to.'

'More than made a claim to,' De Bois snapped back. 'I own it! And if you think you're leaving just like that, you're very much mistaken. There is the matter of you settling your overdue rent.'

'How can we pay you?' said the Elder. 'We have no money.'

'You will work off the debt,' said De Bois curtly.

'I've explained this to you before, but you don't seem to understand what work is.'

'We live on the land with the stegs. We always have done and always will. We don't know how to work for you. It simply cannot be done.'

'That's what you think, is it?' said De Bois, his voice icy. 'In that case, it's a good job I took out an insurance policy this morning.'

The Elder frowned, puzzled.

'What is an insurance policy?'

Hassler chuckled.

'Something to ensure I get from you what I'm owed. Do you know where your children are, Mr Elder?'

'They have already left with the herd, to find new pastures. We are about to follow them. They won't be troubling you.'

'You are correct about one thing – they are with the herd. But you are wrong about *where* they are. At this moment, they are actually heading to the caves under armed escort, where they will be working to pay off your debt to me.'

The elders gasped, shocked. They whispered frantically together.

'You have stolen our children?' the stegosorcerer demanded to know.

De Bois shrugged at the truth.

Inside the hut, Theodore felt rage rising in him. His first instinct was to jump out and attack De Bois, drag him to the caves and force him to free the children. But he didn't know how many men De Bois was using to guard them. The men were armed, De Bois had said as much. And at this moment, Theodore had only one advantage: De Bois didn't know he was there, nor that Bea and Carter were among the children. The best thing he could do was remain hidden, and listen.

'Looking after the stegs is the children's job,' the stegosorcerer proclaimed.

De Bois gave a mocking laugh.

'It seems that like many of the saurs around here, your stegs – sorry, *my* stegs – are worth a lot of money. The children will not need to look after them.'

'You cannot do this!' burst out the Elder. 'The children and those stegs are our life!'

De Bois was obviously enjoying delivering such terrible news, his smirk turning into a broad smile.

'Nothing will go to waste. The meat from them will keep you going while you all work. You should have accepted my first offer. Your pride has cost your tribe dearly.'

'No! There must be another way to settle this,' appealed the Elder.

De Bois shook his head.

'You have left me no option, Mr Elder. Pack up your pathetic huts, load your dirty belongings and make your way to the caves, if you want to be reunited with your children.'

With that, De Bois turned his allosaur around and rode away. As he did, two armed riders, who'd kept out of sight, appeared and rode away alongside him.

Theodore came out of the hut, trembling with rage. The rest of the tribe had now joined the three elders and the stegosorcerer. The women began to wail in sorrow, while the men looked at the elders, dumbstruck and desperate for answers. But Theodore knew there were no easy answers to this dreadful situation. Bea and Carter and the other children were now De Bois' prisoners.

20

A Hard Day's Work

~ an unexpected trump card ~

'I have good news!'

De Bois stood at the entrance to the cave and addressed the children, who'd dismounted from their stegs under the watchful eyes and trained guns of his men. A nasty-looking Ronax chick and a featherless Taku saw that De Bois had returned and sniffed around the children ominously.

'Your tribe know you're with me and they'll be coming to work with you soon.'

'That's good news?' Bea whispered to Sheia.

De Bois gestured at the cave. 'You will do some work for me while they finish packing up your little homes.'

'But we must stay with our stegs and look after them!' protested Sholo.

De Bois laughed.

'Your stegs? I think you mean *my* stegs. You won't be needed to look after them.'

The children looked at one another, bewildered, unable to comprehend what was happening. All they knew was how to look after their stegs.

His men began to push the children towards the mouth of the large cave.

'Boys that side! Girls over here!' shouted De Bois. 'Get them over here!'

Carter jerked away from the man who tried to separate him from Bea.

'You heard him!' barked the man. 'Boys over there!'

The man grabbed Carter's arm and swung him away. Bea reached out and grabbed the man's shirt, and tugged on it hard, making it rip a little. The man let go of Carter and swung around to grab Bea by the wrists, then stopped in surprise.

'Here, Mr De Bois, look what we've got here! A white girl!'

De Bois joined them and looked at Bea, puzzled.

'You're not a Steggi. You don't belong here.'

'Tell him to let go of me,' Bea demanded.

De Bois peered closer at Bea, then said in surprise: 'I know you! You're that girl from the polo club.' To his man, he said, 'Leave her with me. Deal with the others.'

The man released Bea, then went back to shepherding the other children into the cave.

'What are you doing here with the Steggi tribe?' demanded De Bois.

'Just hanging out with friends,' said Bea. She gestured towards Sheia, who was watching, looking concerned.

'These people are not your friends; they are a nuisance,' snapped De Bois. 'Who else are you with?'

'No one,' replied Bea quickly. Too quickly.

De Bois scowled.

'Liar. Where is that little brat who was with you at the polo club? The boy?'

He looked towards the group of boys suspiciously.

'He went back with Theodore last night,' said Bea. 'Some Steggi offered to show them the way. I made a friend and asked to stay for a few days. The tribe was moving on and they said they'd take me back.'

'But what were you all doing with the Steggi in the first place?'

'They saved us. We went to visit the watering hole a day from here. The next day we stumbled upon some poachers who'd killed lots of krugers. The poachers stole our allos, and left us for dead.'

De Bois pulled out his handkerchief, took off his wide-brimmed hat and tried to wipe away the sweat that had oozed from him. Every fold of flab under his clothing gave off a powerful stench of body odour. He dabbed his forehead but it did little to stop the flow of sweat from his brow, as it rolled down his pink flesh and dripped off his podgy nose.

'Poachers, you say?'

He whistled to one of his men and beckoned him over.

'Hedrick, that poacher you found yesterday snooping about.'

'The one we found unconscious in that hole?'

'Yes. What were all the dead saurs lying about there?'

'Krugers, lots of 'em.'

De Bois waved him away then turned back to Bea.

'Your story checks out, at least in part.'

He dabbed at his face again.

'So, you're letting me go?' Bea demanded.

De Bois laughed.

'Oh no, little lady. I've been played an unexpected trump card. You will come in very handy when I get to see Mrs Brownlee again.'

'What does Grandma have to do with this?'

'Possibly, a lot. If I find what I'm looking for in my cave, here on my new estate, then I'll have enough money to buy up all the surrounding land and dig that up as well.'

'And what are you looking for?' demanded Bea.

'Diamonds, of course! What else?' said De Bois. 'In particular, the Queen of Diamonds, a rare and absolutely priceless jewel!'

Bea scoffed.

'"The Queen of Diamonds" is just a stupid story that no one believes.'

'Oh, is that so? Well, let me tell you, young lady, there are diamonds in these caves ...'

'Probably – very tiny ones, not worth very much. Mr Keat showed them to me and my grandmother once.'

'It shows there is a seam of diamonds here, and where there is a seam of small diamonds, there is very likely to be one large one … and I intend to be the one who finds it!'

Bea shook her head.

'You're crazy!' she told him.

De Bois smiled.

'Not me, but the man with whom you will share a cell certainly is.' He signalled to two of his men to come over. 'Put her in with the madman.'

✦ ✦ ✦

Theodore sat beneath the tree, his head in his hands. He was all out of ideas. He played out every move and countermove like a game of chess in his mind, but none of them worked out in a way that would bring all the Steggi children safely back and save the tribe from De Bois. This was De Bois' land. Yes, he'd taken the children prisoner, but in court he would claim it was because of the debt he was owed, a debt that the Steggi could never repay. Theodore knew that money was a powerful weapon, and De Bois had enough of that to get his own way.

Theodore lifted his head at the sound of footsteps approaching. The Steggi were coming, led by the three elders and the stegosorcerer, but now they were dressed for battle. They carried shields made from old steg plates and spears with steg-tail spikes.

'We are going to recover our children,' said the Elder. Theodore looked at them and shook his head sadly.

'It won't work,' he said. 'Your shields may stop a blade, but steg plates are hollow. They won't give you any protection against bullets from a gun. And your spears look threatening, but you'll be shot down long before you can get near enough to use them. Trust me, they'd be more effective attached to a living steg, who could swing its tail around with force. You'll be no match for the rifles of De Bois' men.'

'But we must do something!' burst out the Elder.

'Yes, we must,' agreed Theodore. 'But in a way that ends with you all being alive, you and your children. Which is why I'm thinking.'

The elders and the tribespeople studied Theodore with sad eyes. Finally, the Elder said: 'Please, think quickly.'

Then they turned and walked back to where their dismantled huts and belongings were packed. The stegosorcerer remained with Theodore.

'This has not been as it was foreseen,' he said.

'No, this isn't the way I wanted it,' agreed Theodore.

'I was told to meet a saurman at the sacred tree, and bring a child to the tribe,' said the stegosorcerer.

At this, Theodore stared at the strange man.

'He would bring order to chaos, and free us. Sad the first bit only worked.'

Theodore tried to fit it all into his head, and thought back to the day they met.

'What about the hole? When we met, you had dug a hole to catch someone?'

'To catch bad man, not you,' replied the stegosorcerer. 'Bad men follow good men. You are very important; you brought the child, the child will save the Steggi.'

Theodore sighed.

'I'm not sure if I'm part of the answer,' he said. 'I'm sure haven't been of much help so far—'

He broke off, as they heard an unusual sound high above them, and looked up into the sky. Theodore's face split into a grin, and he clapped his hands together. The *Dragonfly*!

'But that may be about to change! Micki Myers, you beauty. What perfect timing!'

21

Crazy Keat
and the Poacher

~ dealing the pack ~

The cell door squeaked loudly as it ground against the thick metal hinges and slammed shut. Bea pushed herself up from the rock floor where she'd been thrown, and looked around.

The cell was a cage – three sides of barred metal bolted to the fourth wall of bare rock, with more bolts going into the rocky ceiling and floor. A lone candle on the middle metal bar had the residue of other melted candles beneath it, forming a puddle of wax on the floor.

Bea waited until the two men who'd brought her had disappeared around a corner, and she was sure they were heading back through the cavernous passages, before she tried to squeeze between the metal bars – but it was no use, they were set too close together.

She worked her way along the cage, tugging and rattling at every bar and joint and bolt, but all to no avail.

'It's useless,' said a voice. 'Save your strength.'

Alarmed, Bea looked around the cave. In the shadows, she saw a tall, thin, grey-bearded figure. He wore an old, red tartan blanket draped over his ragged clothes, and appeared to be playing a game of Patience with a pack of cards spread out before him on the floor. She recalled De Bois' words about a crazy man.

'Who are you?' she asked, doing her best not to appear frightened, even though she could feel her heart pounding wildly.

His next words stunned her.

'Grace Brownlee? Is that you?'

Bea froze at her mother's name.

'No,' she gulped. Then, summoning her courage, she added: 'Grace was my mother.'

The man moved forward, his face showing his surprise. He was very old, that much Bea could tell.

'Beatrice?' he asked.

Bea was stunned into a moment's silence before she could speak.

'Yes. Who are you?'

The grey-bearded old man came further forward and studied Bea.

'You're just like Grace,' he said.

'Who ... who are you?' repeated Bea.

'Michael Keat. I was an old friend of your grandfather, Sidney.'

'Mr Keat?'

The man nodded. 'I last saw you ...' He thought for a while, trying to remember, before shaking his head sadly and finishing, 'It was a lifetime ago.'

'Grandfather Sidney's funeral?' said Bea. 'I don't properly remember, but I've seen a photograph. You're standing next to Bunty and Ranjit.'

He smiled, and his face seemed to light up in the dimness of the cave. 'Yes! Two names I haven't heard in ages.' He looked at her curiously. 'But what are you doing here?'

Bea sighed. 'It's a long story,' she said.

Keat sat down.

'We have all the time in the world,' he said. 'We can't get out of here.'

Resignedly, and feeling less frightened, Bea sat down next to him on the rocky floor.

'But why are you here?' she asked.

'That villain De Bois,' said Keat. 'He's keeping me here until I tell him where the so-called Queen of Diamonds is. And the others.'

'Other diamonds?'

Keat nodded.

'The Queen was said to be the biggest, but my father told me there were others in the cave that were just as big – a whole pack of them, he said.'

'But surely the Queen of Diamonds is a myth!' said Bea, remembering the strange story De Bois had told them.

'No!' said Keat firmly. 'My father found it. He knew he had to keep the location of the cave a secret. He knew greedy people would come looking for it, but he left me a secret map.'

Bea looked at Keat. *So that's why De Bois calls him crazy,* she thought. *They're both crazy, searching for a diamond which doesn't exist. And not just one imaginary diamond, but a whole seam.*

'What sort of map?' asked Bea, humouring him.

'The cards,' whispered Keat, his voice suddenly so low that Bea could barely make out what he was saying.

'The cards?' said Bea.

Keat nodded. He looked around, as if to make sure they weren't overheard, then pointed at the cards spread out on the floor.

'This pack belonged to my father. He told me they contained a map showing the location of the diamonds,' he whispered.

'How?' she asked.

Keat's face crumpled.

'I don't know,' he moaned. 'My father loved playing cards, often with your grandfather. They played Bridge together. He said he'd tell me the secret, but he never did. I think he was worried in case I might reveal it to someone. But I never would! And then he was killed.'

He looked at the cards.

'I've studied them and studied them, over and over. Examined every card. Laid them out in different orders, different sequences … but the problem is one card is missing from the pack, the queen of diamonds!'

'But if you don't know how to find the map, why is De Bois still keeping you here?'

'Because he doesn't know about the pack of cards, or the secret map.' Keat's voice rose from its whisper in his despair. 'He thinks that I know where the cave is, but I don't!'

He groaned.

'I took De Bois an old diamond my father had kept back. It was found at the same time as the large Queen, but he thinks I found it recently. He cheated me out of it, and my land, in a card game.'

'Yes, Ranjit suggested as much,' said Bea, remembering.

'The only thing keeping me alive is that he thinks I know where the cave is.'

They heard footsteps echo around them and saw a shadow grow large on the opposite wall before a guard turned the corner and came into view. Some small rodents scattered, followed by skinny, thin-legged saurs who had ventured out from their hiding places, looking for a quick bite.

As the guard came closer, a small kink of light lit up the key in his hand.

'Get up!' he barked.

He put the key into the lock, but didn't turn it. Bea and Keat rose to their feet.

'Not you two!' snapped the man. 'The poacher!'

Bea looked about her in confusion, and saw – at the back of the cell, in the dim light – something move, underneath an old blanket.

'Stand up and raise your hands, tough guy. We don't want any more tricks from you.'

Bea looked on, stunned, as a man slowly pulled himself up from beneath the pile of blankets. The poacher's clothes looked oddly smart but were covered in dust and dirt. Suddenly he lunged at the locked door, smashing into it. The force knocked the key to the ground and Bea, instinctively, stamped on it to stop it. The poacher ducked and swiped at Bea's foot as she lifted it, grabbing for it, but it just sent the key spinning further into the cell.

'Give that back!' barked the guard menacingly.

Reluctantly, Bea lifted her foot, but as she was about to pick the key up, the poacher scrambled over and snatched it up first.

'Give it back, I said!' snarled the guard.

The poacher just stood and stared at him defiantly.

'Okay, wise guy, you may have the key, but you're still inside. I'll just wait here till you let yourself out, and then' – he unclipped a bullwhip from his side – 'then I will whip you to within an inch of your life.'

The guard uncoiled the whip and tossed it out a few times, before making an almighty crack with it that echoed through the cavern and scared more small creatures into darting around in all directions.

Another shadow crept along the cave wall from the outside.

'You all right down there, Archie?'

The guard looped his whip up again.

'Sure, just setting out some house rules.'

The poacher hesitated, then tossed the big metal key out of the cell to the guard's feet.

'That's better. Now let's try this again. Stand back, turn around and raise your hands. I'll open this door and you'll step out with your hands held high. Any more tricks, and I'll unleash my whip on you. Got it?'

The poacher nodded, lifted his hands and turned around slowly.

Bea gasped.

Christian Hayter!

22

A New Partnership

~ give him hope ~

'So, I believe I'm addressing a Mr Christian Hayter?' De Bois sat on a rock in the entrance to the cave, and looked inquisitively at Hayter. Hayter stood, his wrists tied behind his back, two of De Bois' men closely guarding him, one with his rifle pointing at their prisoner.

'You've been doing your homework,' grunted Hayter.

'I'm always interested in someone who can seriously injure four of my men before being overpowered.' De Bois reached behind him and produced Hayter's vicious bullhook from where he had hidden it behind the rock. 'A formidable weapon.'

'It's served me well,' said Hayter.

'Perhaps, in Aru and the remote islands you operated in,' said De Bois. He smiled. 'As you say, I've been doing my homework. Your accent, your clothes, the bullhook, all added up to suggest you were not just some common-or-garden local poacher. So I made enquiries of ... certain people. And the name of Christian Hayter – crook, smuggler, recently departed from Aru and rumoured to have travelled to Africa – came up.'

'Is this going to take long?' growled Hayter. 'Now you know who I am, so what?'

'So what indeed?' De Bois replied. 'My name is Hassler De Bois. Out here, on my land, I am justice. Now, I can deal with you as I feel fit, and kill you for poaching on my land, or I can make a proposition to you. One I believe you might find attractive.'

'I'm listening,' said Hayter. He tugged at the ropes binding his wrists. 'But I listen better with my hands free.'

De Bois nodded to his men.

'Untie his wrists. But keep the rifle on him. If he tries anything, shoot him.'

The second guard untied Hayter's wrists.

'I have a job for you, Mr Hayter. I have acquired a number of items that I believe will fetch a good price in the right places abroad.'

'What items?'

'Steg plates.'

Hayter frowned.

'Steg plates can't be exported. Customs won't allow it.'

'I know that, Mr Hayter. I also know, from asking around, that you don't deal with customs.'

Hayter shrugged. 'Maybe, but the price for old ornamental steg plates isn't what it used to be. Sellers need fresh steg plates – they sell to the Far Eastern markets for grinding down into medicine. And they're not so easy to lay your hands on. Not in bulk.'

De Bois nodded thoughtfully.

'Fresh plates sell for more?'

'Much more.'

'How much more?'

'Mr De Bois, you can't get fresh plates,' said Hayter. 'That is why they are priceless.'

'Is that so, Mr Hayter? Please, would you be so kind as to step outside with me?'

De Bois walked out of the cave, followed by Hayter and his two men. At the entrance, they stopped, and De Bois pointed. Hayter's mouth dropped open.

'Stegs!' he exclaimed.

'Exactly,' said De Bois. 'My steg plates are still attached to their previous owners. Is that fresh enough, Mr Hayter?'

'Twenty-six plates per steg,' muttered Hayter, doing a quick calculation. 'There are ten stegs in that herd. That's two hundred and sixty plates!'

'That herd represents just a few of my stegs,' said De Bois. 'I have more on my land.'

'How many more?' asked Hayter.

'At the present count, four hundred,' said De Bois. 'Do we have a deal, Mr Hayter?'

Hayter nodded.

'We certainly do.' He gestured at his once clean,

but now dishevelled, clothes. 'But can we start this new partnership with me getting a bath, a bite to eat and some clean clothes?'

De Bois' expression hardened.

'I did not say anything about a partnership,' he said curtly. 'A partnership would suggest equality. You work for me. You have skills as a smuggler that are useful to me. That's all.'

Hayter looked at him, considering. 'Maybe I've got something else that may be useful to you,' he said.

'What?' asked De Bois.

'Information,' said Hayter. 'You're looking for this big diamond, right? The Queen of Diamonds?

That's why you've got those kids digging in your caves.'

De Bois studied Hayter.

'For someone who's been in a cell for two days, you keep yourself remarkably well informed.'

Hayter tapped his forehead.

'I've got a brain. I've also got ears. That girl you put into the cell. She and the crazy old man were talking. He thought I was asleep. He was telling her about the Queen of Diamonds, and the raw seam in the same cave that's bursting with other diamonds just as big.'

De Bois was alert. His piggy little eyes glittered as he looked at Hayter.

'What did he say?'

'He has a map of where to find them, hidden in a pack of cards that used to belong to his father.'

De Bois' face lit up.

'And where is the cave?' he asked eagerly.

'I don't know,' admitted Hayter. 'All I know is I've seen him playing with the cards, like he's playing a game of Patience or something. He gets them out when I'm asleep, and waits before he hides them again.' He looked enquiringly at De Bois with a smug smile. 'I'm guessing that information's worth something?'

'Perhaps,' agreed De Bois, nodding. 'If you can find out what the secret of the cards is. But to do that, you'll need to become his friend. Get him to trust you.'

'And how do you suggest I do that?' said Hayter sarcastically. 'Give him a present?'

'No, Mr Hayter.' Du Bois smiled, the diamond in his teeth glinting. 'Give him hope.'

23

The Skeleton Key

~ room for just one ~

Michael Keat watched as Bea carefully carved another sliver off the saur bone.

'What are you doing?' he asked.

'Making a skeleton key,' replied Bea. She chuckled. 'In this case, from a real skeleton.' At the back of the cave, she'd found the bones of a small oviraptor, which had been thrown there after the meat was eaten. She'd selected a bone that included the flat shoulder blade and had been working on it, filing it against a sharp part of the cage bars. She put the carved bone alongside an impression in the puddle of soft candle wax, which had accidentally been made when she had stamped on the key.

'I saw it in one of Monty's movies,' Bea explained. 'He – or, rather, Monty's character – made an impression of a key in wax, and then made a copy so they could get out of the cell they were being held in.'

She made a last incision in the bone, and placed it gently into the impression.

'It fits!' she said delightedly. 'Now all we have to do is hope it works when we put it into the lock. It's an old bone, so it might break.'

They heard a noise from outside. Immediately, Bea stuffed the bone key into her pocket, and moved to the back of the cave. Hayter appeared, pushed roughly by the guard who'd taken him out before. Another guard was with them. This one pointed his rifle at Hayter as the first unlocked the cell door.

Hayter was pushed into the cell, and the door slammed shut and locked. As the guards disappeared, Hayter dropped to the ground and held his ribs, groaning.

'The swines nearly killed me!' he moaned.

Bea watched him carefully. She had no love for this man and she had a million questions as to why he was here, but she hated to see anyone suffer.

'What did they want?' she asked.

'Who knows?' groaned Hayter. 'I think they just wanted to amuse themselves by beating me up.' Painfully, he pushed himself up off the ground. 'But I did find out one thing. De Bois is going to kill us.'

'Kill us?' echoed Bea, horrified.

Hayter nodded. 'I heard him tell the guards. He thinks you'll bring trouble, and the old man's worthless. But I've got a plan to get out of here.'

'What is it?' asked Keat.

Hayter shook his head.

'Room for just one in this plan.'

'Typical!' snorted Bea.

'Listen, kid, it's every man for himself,' snapped Hayter. He looked at them thoughtfully, then added: 'Unless it's worth my while, of course.'

'You want payment?' scoffed Bea. She gestured at herself and Keat. 'Look at us! You think we've got money?'

'Maybe not here, but your grandmother has money to spare. Maybe we could do a deal over something.' He looked at Keat. 'And these giant diamonds you're always going on about. A share of that might be worth it. What do you say?'

'Don't trust him!' said Bea quickly. 'I bet he hasn't even got a plan!'

'Well, that shows how little you know, young lady,' smirked Hayter. He pulled a pistol from the back of his trousers and placed it on the floor. 'Luckily, I'm also a good pickpocket.'

Bea stared at the gun, impressed, but then her face clouded. 'Nice idea, but a pistol only has six bullets, and there are more than six armed men out there. Besides, you may shoot us with it.'

Hayter grinned.

'I might just do that, but you have a value, and' – he smiled – 'so does this'. He pulled a key from his back pocket.

Bea looked at it closely and then back at Hayter, who was grinning from ear to ear.

'We have a—' began Keat, but Bea cut him off before he could finish.

'A key and a gun, great work, Mr Hayter,' she said quickly. 'So why exactly do you need us?'

'Well, like I said, I'm interested in these diamonds. Tell me how to find them, and maybe we can do a deal to get out of here.' He grinned. 'So, what do you say? Where are the diamonds?'

'We're still working on that,' said Bea. She didn't trust him yet – but he clearly believed the story about the diamonds, so perhaps it was worth keeping him interested.

'Well, let me know when you've worked it out,' said Hayter, shrugging. 'I'll leave later, when there are fewer guards. Until then I'm going back to sleep. De Bois and his men gave me a rough time.'

Keat and Bea watched Hayter as he went back to the bundle of rags in the corner and pulled them over himself, disappearing from view.

'Why didn't you tell him about the key you made?' Keat whispered. 'We can use it to get out.'

Bea shook her head and spoke very quietly into his ear.

'I don't trust him. Hayter's evil and vicious, and he lies. If we told him about our key, he'd simply take it and escape, and leave us here, locked in.'

'But he has his own key!' Keat whispered back.

'Well, it's a key all right,' whispered Bea. 'But it's not the one to the cage we're in!'

◆ ◆ ◆

Night fell. The only light in the cell was that from a stub of candle, the flame flickering, throwing eerie shadows. Bea sat by the spread of cards, studying them. The answer was here somewhere, she knew. But where?

She looked towards Hayter, asleep beneath the pile of rags, then moved to where Michael Keat sat.

'Are you ready?' she whispered.

He nodded and gathered up the cards in a cloth, making a small bundle.

'The cards,' he said. 'That's all I need.'

'Okay,' said Bea. 'I've decided we also have to take Hayter with us.'

'But you said he's dangerous,' said Keat.

'He is, but he has a gun, and somehow we're on the same side against De Bois. If we take him with us, maybe he'll create a diversion, giving us a chance to escape and free Carter and the others.'

'How?' asked Keat.

'I don't know that yet,' admitted Bea.

She moved across to the pile of rags and poked it.

'Hayter,' she said. 'I know you're awake.'

There was a grunt from beneath the rags, then they were pulled back and Hayter poked his head out.

'What?' he growled.

'Let's go,' said Bea. 'I've got a key to the door.'

Hayter sat up, immediately alert, checking his pockets and pulling out the key he'd shown them. 'You're lying. I have the key right here.'

'Your key opens something, but not this cage,' said Bea. 'Right now, your only chance is with me. We'll leave together, but once we're out, you go your own way.'

Hayter moved to the door and put his key into the lock, then swore as he realised it didn't fit.

'Okay,' he grunted. He looked at the bundle Keat was holding. 'Let me guess – those stupid cards of yours?'

Keat didn't answer. He and Hayter followed Bea to the cell door. She inserted the key into the lock.

'Is that bone?' asked Hayter.

Bea nodded.

'It'll break as soon as it comes under pressure,' said Hayter.

'You got a better idea?' asked Bea.

Hayter grunted, and watched as Bea slowly turned the key. The key stopped turning as it hit the lever mechanism.

Please, let it work! Bea prayed silently.

Gently, she increased the pressure on the key, a bit at a time, as she tried to turn it in the lock.

Please, don't let it snap!

She applied a bit more pressure, and suddenly there was a click, and the door swung open. It had worked!

'Let's go!' said Bea exultantly.

As she stepped through, she found her arm grabbed in a strong grip, and a pistol shoved in her back.

'Guards!' shouted Hayter. 'Call De Bois! Tell him I've got the cards!'

24

The Secret of the Map

~ the missing card ~

De Bois had obviously been roused from his bed, because when his men thrust Bea, Keat and Hayter into the large communal tent, He appeared wearing an ornate light-pink dressing gown and gold slippers, both adorned with small diamonds. Bea thought he looked more than ever like a pig.

He stood surveying the three of them, coldly.

'This had better be good,' he said, threateningly.

Hayter gestured at the small bundle Keat was clinging on to.

'There,' said Hayter. 'The cards you were after.'

'He's told you the secret of the map?' asked De Bois eagerly.

'No,' said Hayter. 'But that's because he doesn't know. But she' – he gestured at Bea – 'she was playing with them, and she had a look on her face. I've got a good idea she knows the secret.'

'Do you?' De Bois, suddenly alert, threw the question at Bea.

I have to be careful, Bea realised. *If I say no, then there's no reason for him to keep me alive. But if I say yes, he'll insist I tell him.*

'I think I know,' she said slowly.

'Do you or don't you?' shouted De Bois. The idea of being so near to discovering the diamonds was infuriating him.

'I've got an idea, and I'm working on it,' said Bea. Buying time, she added: 'I think I'm close.'

'I told you!' smirked Hayter.

'She could be lying,' said De Bois, frowning. Then he gave an evil smile. 'There's one way to find out. I'm holding a lot of Steggi children on my estate, young lady. If you want no harm to come to your "friends", you'll come up with the answer.'

There was a sudden commotion in the hallway, and two men burst into the room. Between them they were holding the struggling figure of Carter, who was writhing in their grasp and kicking out at them with his bare feet. De Bois stared at them, shocked.

'What are you doing bringing that filthy Steggi creature here?' he demanded. 'He's covered in ash and dung!'

'He tried to escape, sir,' said one of the guards, who had a ripped shirt and deep bite marks up his arm. 'We had to overpower him, and as we did, some of the ash fell off, and we found that he's not a Steggi. Underneath, he's white. Like the girl.'

'What?'

Before De Bois could get up and march across to the struggling boy, Carter spotted Hayter standing behind Bea grinning from ear to ear. A deep hatred boiled up in the boy and when De Bois came close enough Carter burst from the men and kicked at the portly pig-like man in an attempt to leap over him and strike at Hayter. Strike first to get the advantage – it was the shadow raptor way. The guards were not quick enough, but Hayter was. He held De Bois safely aside and lashed out with his bullhook, stopping just short of Carter's face so that the downturned hook pressed coldly against his cheek.

The guards righted themselves and grabbed Carter. Hayter moved De Bois back into control and signalled for him to continue.

De Bois nodded his appreciation to his new friend and looked back to the boy whilst clearing his thoughts. He slowly leant in a little more carefully and wiped the ash off Carter's head and face, then broke into a broad smile as he saw Bea's horrified expression.

'Well, look who it is!' He turned to Bea. 'So, he didn't leave after all. How fortunate! This is even better. Now you have a real incentive to crack the code. If you don't by sunrise, my men will kill him.'

He scowled as Carter aimed a kick at him, narrowly missing.

'And you can start by getting him to behave himself, or I'll have my men shoot him right now.'

'Carter! Be good!' burst out Bea.

Carter stopped struggling and looked questioningly at his sister.

Bea nodded. 'It'll be all right,' she said. 'I promise.'

Carter glared at the men holding him, but, trusting his sister, his struggles subsided.

'Good,' said De Bois. 'You seem to have some control over this wild thing. Right, I'm off back to my tent and to bed. Hayter, you'll stay here and keep an eye on them all while the young lady gets to work to discover the mystery of the cards.' He turned to Bea and added pointedly: 'Find the location of the cave where the Queen of Diamonds was discovered.' He gestured at Carter as he told his men: 'If the boy tries anything, shoot him. Just enough to damage him. A bullet in the leg will be fine. But I need him alive, for the moment.'

Hayter looked to De Bois and struck his bullhook into his hand menacingly.

'And get my new associate some food and drink.'

With that, De Bois swept out.

Hayter grinned nastily at Bea.

'Looks like you're going to have a busy night,' he said.

Hayter reached out for the bundle Keat was holding. Keat hugged his precious cards tighter to his chest, but

Hayter punched him in the face, sending the old man reeling back. Keat fell to the floor, and Hayter snatched the bundle from him.

'Put him in a chair,' he told one of the men. 'If he moves, shoot him.' He pointed at Carter. 'Same for that one.'

The guards took Carter to an armchair under a lantern and dumped him in it.

'Be good, be good, Carter,' Bea urged him.

Hayter tipped out the bundle onto the table.

'Over to you, kid.' He smirked at Bea. 'And, for your sake, I hope you come up with the answer.'

◆ ◆ ◆

Bea sat at the trestle table. Keat and Carter sat in their fold-out chairs, looking at the armed men who stood guard over them, and at Bea as she studied the cards she'd laid out on the table. Hayter was at the far end of the table, with a plate of sandwiches in front of him, which he munched on greedily as he, too, watched Bea.

'I've changed my mind,' Hayter said. 'I hope you don't work it out. I hope De Bois kills you. You've caused me a lot of grief.'

Bea glared at him.

'You double-crossed us,' she hissed. 'I should have left you in the cell to rot.'

'I wasn't asleep,' smirked Hayter. 'I was listening the whole time. I guessed you were up to something.'

'What I would like to know is why you were in a cell here in Kenya and not rotting in a cell all the way back in Indonesia?' asked Bea.

Hayter wiped his lips with his sleeve and chuckled to himself. 'Yes, strange, isn't it? Perhaps you should turn around more often; I've been following you.'

'Why?' Bea snapped.

'Why not?' Hayter snapped back, slamming his fist on the table and making the cards jump. 'Right now, I would be thinking more about your short future, and not the past, young lady.'

Bea turned her attention back to the cards and tried desperately to remember the various card games her grandfather had taught her. The picture cards: king, queen, jack. Was there something in the way they had been drawn? Something in one particular king, say, that wasn't there in the others? A difference in the number of jewels in their crowns? She examined the number cards, comparing the four suits: hearts, diamonds, spades and clubs. Was there something special in the way the numbers had been set out? Was one card different from the rest?

Time passed – first in long minutes, then stretching to hours – and still, nothing revealed itself to her. It was just a pack of cards.

Suddenly she remembered what Michael Keat had said about his father promising to tell him the secret.

What else had he said? He used to play Bridge all the time with … That could be it! Bridge!

Frantically, she struggled to recall her grandfather Sidney trying to teach her the rules of the game. Everything about it had seemed so complicated, and she'd been too young to want to play such a complex game. But could it help her find the answer?

She turned the cards face down. There were dull scratch marks on the backs of them all that she'd assumed had been made by long years of being carried and hidden by Michael Keat. But when she looked at them closely now, they suddenly looked like they were part of a pattern. She looked at three of the cards and saw that the apparently random scratches on the backs of them joined up. *Was it a coincidence?* She turned the three cards over and saw that they were the three, four and five of hearts.

Carefully – she didn't want Hayter to realise her discovery – she picked up a few of the cards, and ran her fingers slowly over them. Yes, they all had it, the same scratches!

The tent doorway was pulled aside, letting in the morning light and De Bois stepped in. He was fully dressed now.

'Well?' he demanded. 'Has she cracked the code yet?'

'No,' scowled Hayter.

'Yes,' retorted Bea.

De Bois, Hayter and Keat all stared at her, stunned. Carter was still trying to understand what was so important about all the cards.

'What did you say?' demanded De Bois.

'I said yes. I've cracked it. I think I know what the code is,' said Bea.

'Why didn't you say so?' shouted Hayter, furious. He turned to De Bois and appealed: 'She didn't say anything about this before you came in. She's bluffing!'

'I've only just worked it out,' said Bea.

'Well?' demanded De Bois impatiently, ignoring Hayter. 'What is it?'

'The key is the game of Bridge,' said Bea.

She began to lay the cards out in numerical order by suit: hearts, diamonds, clubs then spades, all facing upwards.

'Watch,' she said.

One by one, she turned them all over until the back of the cards were staring up at them, and now the pattern made by the scratches was clear. It was a kind of map, but it wasn't quite right. It was disjointed, scrambled.

Suddenly she seemed to hear her grandfather's voice explaining the game to her all those years ago, and she realised what was wrong. The numerical order was right but not the suit order.

Swiftly she swapped around a few kings and aces and, before their eyes, the pattern scratched into the cards took shape. The code was finally broken. The map was revealed.

'Perfect!' breathed De Bois.

'No, it isn't,' said Hayter. He gestured at a gap in the centre of the cards laid out on the table. 'There's a card missing.'

De Bois smiled.

'The missing card is the proof that this is the answer,' he said. 'The missing card is the queen of diamonds. The cards are a map of this very landscape. Look!' De Bois pointed to his own map. 'It all lines up!'

Then he pointed at the gap in the cards, with a shaking finger.

'The missing queen of diamonds is where we find the cave!'

25

The Queen of Diamonds

~ the hare-brained plan ~

De Bois examined his map as he studied the huge rockface pitted with caves. Hayter hovered beside him, his beady eyes watchful, while Bea, Carter and Keat were kept at a distance by the armed guards. Some way off, the Steggi children stood outside one of the caves they had been bundled into to sleep and with their armed guards were wondering why all the attention was now over there. Sholo tried to slip away as everyone looked on but had been battered to the ground by one of the guards with the butt of a rifle. A short distance away, the giant stegs grunted, restless: their morning routine was not as it should be and without the application of ash clay the bugs were biting and the sun was hot.

'That one!' shouted De Bois, pointing.

Followed by Hayter and his men, he ran to the cave and stopped at the entrance.

'It's blocked,' he said.

'There's been a rockfall,' said Hayter. 'You can see where the roof and the sides have caved in. It must have happened after old man Keat found the Queen. That's why he never went back to get the rest. It'll need explosives to open it up.

'It's still not going to be easy finding the diamonds,' said Hayter. 'There'll be tons of rock to go through once that blast opens up the cave.'

'That's what the Steggi children are going to do,' said De Bois. 'Those small hands of theirs are perfect for sorting through small pieces of rubble.' He turned and shouted at his guards. 'Take the girl and the other two back to the cell and lock them in!'

'Be careful, they're tricky,' said Hayter. 'Last time she made a key so she could get out.'

'I was going to ask how you got out with the wrong key,' De Bois chuckled.

Hayter scowled and gritted his teeth as he glared at De Bois.

'The girl could be lying,' he cautioned. 'It could be just another empty cave.'

'No,' said De Bois. 'Diamonds are my life. I can smell them. Feel their presence. I knew they were here somewhere!'

Suddenly there was a warning shout from one of his men.

'We've got company, boss!'

A buzzing noise from the sky made them all look up. A red biplane was circling in the sky above them. There was smoke coming from it and its engine was making spluttering sounds.

'It looks like it's in trouble, and coming in to land, boss!'

De Bois pointed at the Steggi children.

'Get those kids and the stegs under cover!' he shouted. 'Move them into the caves so they can't be seen! Put them in the big cavern. Do it now!!'

◆ ◆ ◆

Carter had stopped when he heard the sound of the plane's engine, and looked up at the sky. He recognised the tone and pitch of the *Dragonfly* instantly and smiled.

'Move!' snarled one of the guards, jabbing him with his rifle.

Bea had recognised the plane as well.

'Come on, Carter,' she said. 'Let's not cause trouble.'

Not just yet, she added to herself determinedly, as they headed for the cave and the cell. If, as she hoped, Micki Myers had come to help them, there'd be trouble soon enough.

◆ ◆ ◆

De Bois' men hurried to carry out his orders, first locking Bea, Carter and Keat into the cage, then shepherding the children and the stegs into a huge cavernous space in the rocks set behind the cage. The cooler, damp air and shade were a relief from the searing heat outside. The Steggi children, happy to be reunited with their stegs, did not let on that this large cave was well known to them, and that they visited it once a year. The great cavern walls were covered in a salty residue the stegs licked to top up vital minerals in their sparse diet of dry bush.

De Bois and Hayter watched the plane. It continued to circle, but there was no mistaking it was in trouble. They could hear the engine coughing and smoke continued to streak from its engine, until finally it came down on a flat area of ground, some distance from the nest of caves, close to where the rocky outcrop began, along with a small wooded area of thin trees and shrubs. It bounced a few times before settling to the ground, smoke billowing out from the engine. The plane stalled, backfired and jolted to a stop.

'Hedrick, go and tell him this area's out of bounds,' De Bois ordered. 'Get rid of him.'

Hedrick hurried to the plane, reaching it as the dust blew away and the pilot jumped out.

'You're not allowed to land here,' he said.

Micki removed her leather helmet and swung her long locks out.

'So sorry, I'm having a spot of bother.'

Hedrick's mouth dropped open and he stared at her.

'You're a woman!' he burst out.

'Ten out of ten for observation,' said Micki. 'Thank goodness you're here. I think a bird flew into the engine and caught alight.' She went around and opened up the nacelles that covered the engine, which let out more smoke. 'Yep, that's what's left of it.'

She tentatively pulled out a smoking clump of steg dung and tossed it to the floor, leaving her glove smouldering.

'I'm going to need some water. Be a darling and get some, would you?'

◆ ◆ ◆

De Bois looked annoyed as Hedrick returned.

'Why's he still here?' he demanded. 'I told you to get rid of him.'

'He's actually a she, boss,' said Hedrick apologetically. 'And she's got a problem with her plane. It caught fire. She needs some water.'

◆ ◆ ◆

Micki leant into the cockpit and whispered to Theodore and Monty, who were squashed behind the pilot's seat. 'It looks like the big boss is on his way. I'll get rid of him and then you two can get out. I've parked near some bushes and rocks to give you cover.'

'Good day!' called a booming voice. 'I am Hassler De Bois. I understand you're having trouble.'

Micki climbed down from the wing and smiled radiantly at the portly man. He held a water caddy out to her. 'My man said you needed some water.'

'Thank you!' beamed Micki. She took the caddy and poured some of it over the plane's engine, which let off a plume of steam. 'That's done the trick. I just need to replace a few burnt-out parts. Luckily I have spares.' She kicked the tyre next to her and said thoughtfully, 'I could do with a better take-off than my landing, though. I can't afford to lose a wheel or I'll be stuck here. Would you be an absolute darling and have your men clear a runway for me?'

Once again she gave him the full impact of her smile. De Bois responded with a bow and a smile of his own.

'Certainly, dear lady. It will be my pleasure.'

He turned and headed back, ready to bark the orders at his men.

'Okay,' muttered Micki. 'Now's your chance.'

She poured the rest of the caddy over the engine, creating an even bigger cloud of steam.

♦ ♦ ♦

Theodore and Monty used the opportunity to scramble out of the cockpit, then hurried to the cover nearby. They made their way towards the nest of caves, keeping out of sight behind the rocks. Fortunately, as Micki had intended, most of De Bois' men were now occupied in clearing the ground.

Theodore and Monty found a hidden spot from where they could observe everything. They watched as Micki examined the area the men had cleared as a runway, pointing out smaller stones that could do 'all sorts of damage', which the men seemed happy to pick up and move aside. When they got to the end she sighed and explained it had to be twice as long.

'Otherwise I might not get the lift I need to take off, and if I don't, and I crash, I'll be here for ages.'

'She's milking this a bit,' muttered Theodore.

'Men will do crazy things for a woman's attention,' Monty commented.

Theodore looked at him with an eyebrow raised.

'Like come on a hare-brained rescue mission?'

♦ ♦ ♦

Finally, the engine that was never broken was 'fixed'; the 'bird' on fire was now steg-dung ash, blowing around in the wind; and there was a pristine runway from which to take off.

Micki waved at all the men and blew De Bois a

poisonous little kiss, before letting the propeller blow a
cloud of dry dirt all over them as she headed down the
extra-long runway. A loop-the-loop kept them glued to
her for as long as possible, giving Theodore and Monty
more time to put the next part of the hare-brained plan
into action.

◆ ◆ ◆

De Bois stood waving for a long time, until he was certain
she was properly gone.

'She won't tell anyone we're digging here, boss, will
she?' asked Hedrick.

De Bois smirked. 'No chance. That pretty little woman
had no idea what's going on. Now, let's get to work. Start
packing the explosives inside that cave entrance.'

✦ ✦ ✦

Theodore and Monty peered over the rocks at the scene.

'What are they taking into that cave?' asked Monty.

'Explosives,' replied Theodore. 'They're going to do some blasting.' His eyes took in the rest. 'No sign of Bea or Carter, or the Steggi kids and the stegs.'

'He must have hidden them somewhere,' said Monty. 'Possibly when he saw Micki's plane coming into land?'

'That's what I'm thinking,' agreed Theodore. 'The question is, where?'

Suddenly he stiffened as a familiar-looking man came out of the cave, and picked up a box of explosives. He turned so his face was visible, and paused before carrying it back in.

'Hayter!' burst out Theodore, shocked.

'Who?' asked Monty.

'Christian Hayter. An evil and extremely vicious villain,' said Theodore. 'What's he doing here?'

Theodore was so enraged by the sight of Hayter, just standing there, that he was distracted, his mind whirring. Then a sudden movement by one entrance to a cave, some distance from all the action, caught his eye. Two men, both armed with rifles, had appeared from within and were now sitting down outside it. But Theodore noticed they weren't relaxed; both were alert, and kept shooting looks back into the cave.

'Why are those two so far from the action?' he mused.

'It looks to me like they're guarding something in that cave,' said Monty.

'I'm guessing it's something important,' observed Theodore. He looked at Monty with a smile. 'Ever played a villain before?'

'What do you mean?'

'In your films. You know, all the ladies secretly fancy the bad guy.'

'No,' said Monty firmly. 'They may fancy the bad guy, but the hero always gets the girl.'

'Okay, what about a hero who has to pretend to be a bad guy, in order to rescue children?'

Monty grinned. 'Now you're talking my language! What's my motivation?'

'You need to win the heart of a very attractive woman … who's a pilot.'

'All right.' Monty nodded. 'I'm motivated.'

26

Stampede of Stegs

– hell for leather –

Theodore trudged towards the two guards outside the cave, with his hands behind his head and a gloomy expression on his face. Monty walked behind him, his rifle pointed at Theodore's back. The two guards rose to their feet as the other pair neared them.

'What's this?' demanded one.

'I found him sneaking about like a rat, while on patrol,' said Monty in an exaggerated accent. 'The boss said to lock him up.'

One of the guards nodded and produced a key.

'Probably looking for the other poacher. We'll put him with the other prisoners. Follow me,' he said, and turned to enter the cave.

Thwack! Theodore's fist swung, and the guard collapsed. Monty swung his rifle and hit the other just a second later, sending him crashing to the ground too.

'Wow! It never goes to plan in the movies!' exclaimed Monty.

✦ ✦ ✦

Bea watched the shadows on the opposite wall grow. The guards were coming.

Two men appeared, dragging two bodies with them. Then one of the guards took off his hat and looked in at her, a broad grin on his face. The other man ran to join him.

'Theodore! Monty!' burst out Bea. She and Carter rushed to the bars. 'You were in Micki's plane?'

'We were indeed,' said Theodore, putting the key in the lock. 'We'll talk later. Right now, let's get you out of there.'

The door swung open and the children hurled themselves at Monty and Theodore, hugging them with relief and delight. Theodore became aware of the ragged old man approaching them, a look of wonder on his face.

'Is that Theodore Logan?' he asked, his voice trembling.

'Michael Keat!' exclaimed Theodore. 'This is where you disappeared to.'

'De Bois lied,' said Bea.

'Yes, we gathered that,' said Theodore. 'Where are the children and the stegs? We're here to get you all out.'

'Deeper in this cave, in a larger cavern beyond this.'

'Are there guards with them?'

'I don't think so,' said Bea. She gestured at the two unconscious men. 'I think these two were supposed to guard the entrance for all of us.'

'Good,' said Theodore. 'Okay. The plan is to get the stegs to run out of the cave with you and the kids on them, and go hell for leather. That should take De Bois and his men by surprise.' He patted the rifle he was holding. 'I'll bring up the rear to make sure no one comes after you. Monty, you go with the kids and the stegs.'

'Got you.' Monty nodded.

Theodore turned to Bea and said to her firmly: 'And make sure that once you start, you keep going. The important thing is for you all to get away from here and get free.'

'Got it,' said Bea.

Carter looked at her and Theodore inquisitively. Bea saw his confusion and outlined the shape of a large steg with her hands, then mimed mounting it.

'We ride stegs,' she said. 'All of us. Shola, Sheia, you, me. All.'

She pointed into an imaginary distance.

'We ride far away.'

Carter grinned.

'Far away,' he echoed. 'From bad men.'

'Yes!' beamed Bea.

'Just make sure you keep the stegs away from the cave with the explosives,' said Theodore. 'It's the one ...'

'I know which one it is,' said Bea grimly. 'I found it for him.'

'You can explain it all later,' Theodore said. 'We need to put these characters somewhere safe first.'

He and Monty dragged the unconscious guards into the cell, then locked it. That done, they all went deeper into the cave together. They turned a corner in the narrow tunnels and suddenly found themselves in a massive cavern, as if a huge underground cathedral had been carved out of the rock. The herd of stegs had been corralled inside, and with them were Shola, Sheia and the other Steggi children.

At the sight of Bea, Carter and Theodore, Shola and Sheia let out cries of delight, and ran over, throwing their arms around them.

'Time for that later,' said Theodore. 'Right now, we go. Escape. Take the stegs and get away.'

'Yes,' beamed Shola. He turned to the children and gave a whistle, and they all mounted their stegs, who appeared refreshed from the salt and shade.

Theodore looked at the frail figure of Michael Keat.

'Mr Keat, you're best sticking with me. Holding onto a charging steg is tricky, and anyway, we adults aren't allowed on them. 'Will you manage to keep up?'

'I have to,' said Keat. 'It's either that or stay here as a prisoner. I'll take my chances with you.'

'Okay,' said Theodore. He looked up at the children atop their stegs. 'Let's roll!'

✦ ✦ ✦

De Bois and Hayter watched as the last of the
explosives were placed just inside the entrance
of the diamond cave, where the rockfall had
sealed off the cave itself. Lengths of fuse wire had
been rolled out, and the explosives connected to a
detonator.

'That should do it!' De Bois called to his men. 'Get
back and take cover!'

He was just heading towards the detonator when a
shout of alarm made him swing around. Stegs were
pouring out of the prisoners' cave, their tails
swinging wildly, children riding atop the
entire herd, which was headed straight

towards De Bois' men. Caught unawares, some were smashed down by the tails and crumpled to the ground. Others couldn't get out of the way fast enough, and were trampled beneath the huge creatures' feet. De Bois and Hayter heard shooting, and turned to see Theodore, Keat and Monty running behind the stampeding stegs, firing into the air, driving the stegs onwards and adding to the panic.

'Logan!' raged Hayter.

De Bois stared at what was happening in a state of shock. Suddenly everything was out of his control, and he was a man used to being firmly *in* control. His men, who a moment earlier had been stacking explosives, were now fleeing before the stampeding stegs.

'Get back!' he shouted at them. He snatched up a fallen rifle and swung it around, but the speed of the stampeding stegs had taken most of them past him. Desperate to get out of the path of the other stegs, he ran for the cover of the cave, Hayter close behind him.

Carter pulled his steg back. Bea, Sholo, Sheia and the others had got away, but Carter was remembering his days as one of the raptor clan. When the tribe fled before predators, the slowest had to be protected. The old man, Mr Keat, was the slowest. Theodore was staying alongside Mr Keat.

'Go!' shouted Theodore at Carter.

But Carter was determined to remain close and protect them.

BANG!

A bullet smashed into the rocks by Theodore, sending chips of stone flying. Carter looked at where the shot had come from, and saw De Bois just inside the cave, steadying the rifle for another shot.

BANG! The second shot flew over Carter's head.

Carter pulled his steg around, to try to give Theodore protection.

BANG!

The bullet hit Carter's steg in the head, and as Theodore watched in horror, the huge animal staggered, then collapsed.

Carter rolled off just before the steg hit the ground,

then threw himself behind a rock, as De Bois fired again.

Theodore left Keat in the cover of some rocks and ran towards Carter and the fallen steg. Bullets from De Bois' gun smashed into the ground and the rocks around him. Theodore reached the fallen steg, at the same time as Carter dived from behind the rocks to join him. Carter leant gently against the steg. It was breathing, but its lungs were making a fluting sound, a dreadful, low strangled wail.

BANG!

The sound of the shot seemed to stir the steg, and it struggled upwards, pushing itself to its feet. Theodore moved back to give the huge creature room, and as he did so he saw the tall box of the detonator for the explosives, barely two feet away from them … and its plunger handle, which had been left up, ready for action.

'Look out!' he began to shout, but it was too late.

The steg crumpled, staggering sideways, and it fell, crunching down on the detonator. As Theodore saw it hit the plunger, he grabbed Carter —

27

Respects to the Fallen

~ time to go ~

*B*OOOOMMMMM!!!!

Theodore and Carter took refuge behind the bulk of the dead steg, as huge flying rocks exploded into its body, and clouds of thick dust settled over them. Theodore pulled his jacket over their heads to give them some protection and prevent them from suffocating. The ground shook, and smaller rocks rained down on them.

Finally, when the ground had stopped shaking and the clouds of dust seemed to have eased, Theodore let his jacket down, and they looked out at the scene.

The cave had disappeared completely. Where De Bois had been standing was now a massive rockfall of boulders.

They found Michael Keat looking barely recognisable, covered from head to foot in rock dust. Miraculously, the rocks he'd been hiding behind had protected him from the flying boulders. As Theodore and Carter helped him to his feet and began to shake the dust off him, they heard the sound of the stegs returning. They turned to see Bea,

Shola and Sheia leading the other children back, with Monty running behind.

Bea leapt off her steg and ran to Carter, hugging him tight.

'We heard the explosion,' she said. 'I was so worried, Carter!'

'We're safe,' Theodore reassured her. He gestured to where Carter's steg lay almost hidden by rocks. 'Sadly, Carter's steg didn't make it. De Bois shot him, and in doing so he signed his own death warrant.' He pointed at the rockfall that completely obscured the cave. 'The steg set off the detonator. That's the end of De Bois.'

'And Hayter?' asked Bea.

'When I last saw him, he was there with De Bois, so I guess both of them caught it.' He scowled. 'Now we'll never know what Hayter was doing here.'

Monty looked towards the huge pile of rocks where the cave had been.

'It looks like De Bois was finally united with his precious diamonds,' he said.

'Hullu! Hullu!'

The shouts made them turn, and with whoops of joy the children saw their parents had arrived, dressed for battle in steg plates, and carrying spears. The children ran to the adults, throwing themselves into their arms, while the stegosorcerer and the elders headed towards Theodore, Carter, Bea and Monty. The Elder took Theodore's hand and looked at him with an intense gaze.

'You did it, my friend,' he said. 'You said you would free our children, and you did. You and your companions.' He looked at Bea and Carter and Monty. 'You will always be welcome among the Steggi.'

'We're honoured,' said Theodore humbly. With a saddened look he pointed the dead steg. 'But I'm afraid one of the stegs died. Killed by the bad man.'

The Elder looked towards the dead creature and nodded.

'We will honour our friend,' he said. He looked towards the stegosorcerer, who suddenly gave a loud ululating wail that echoed around the site. Everyone stopped, and watched as the stegosorcerer walked towards the fallen steg. Then, realising what had happened, they followed him.

'This is where we pay our respects to the fallen,' whispered Theodore.

'What do we do?' asked Bea, feeling helpless.

'We do nothing, except stand with them and honour the ceremony,' said Theodore.

Bea, Carter, Mr Keat and Monty followed Theodore, and they joined the Steggi standing in a circle around the fallen steg, which was half buried beneath rocks and boulders. They stood in respectful silence with the Steggi as the stegosorcerer carried out the ceremony, moving gracefully around the fallen steg, gesticulating with his arms and his staff, as he chanted and sang. Gradually the Steggi joined in his chanting and singing, at first in low harmonious voices, which then built into a beautiful choir of celebration.

After the ceremony, the Steggi worked together to heap more rocks onto the fallen steg, to complete the burial.

'That was so moving,' whispered Bea, wiping her eyes.

Keat's eyes strayed towards the rockfall where De Bois and Hayter had perished. He gave a deep sigh. 'My father's diamonds have gone.'

'Will you try to dig for them?' asked Theodore.

Keat shook his head. 'They've already caused too much tragedy. Let them stay buried.'

Theodore nodded, then asked, 'Then come with us back to the Brownlee lodge'.

Keat looked around and the carnage and sighed. 'Can you and Bunty help me with lawyers?'

'Why, Ranjit certainly can,' Theodore replied.

'Good, I need to make sure this land never falls into the wrong hands again. My father bought it because he found the cave with diamonds, but that's what eventually killed him. It feels like I have finally been freed of the same curse … Will Bunty take my land and join the estates? Perhaps I can keep my old house?'

Theodore looked amazed at his offer, but shook his head. 'I'm afraid Bunty could not afford it, Michael.'

'I'm not selling it, I'm giving it!' Keat blurted out. 'Send word to Ranjit Bapat that I'm alive and in need of a lawyer!'

Theodore agreed, and then became aware of the stegosorcerer approaching them. He bowed his head to him.

'A beautiful ceremony,' he said.

'For a beautiful creature with a beautiful heart,' replied the stegosorcerer.

'Which is more than could be said for the two who died there,' said Theodore, looking at the rockfall. 'It looks like we caught your bad man, after all!'

The stegosorcerer looked thoughtful.

'It seems so, but still I see a bad man in a hole. And fire.'

'Fire?' asked Theodore. 'Where? What sort of fire? The fire-walking?'

'Maybe he means the fire of the explosion?' suggested Bea.

The stegosorcerer shook his head.

'I do not know,' he said. 'But the bad man and the fire are one.'

'Thanks,' said Theodore. 'We've been warned.' He turned to Bea and Carter. 'I think we need to get going, kids. It's a long journey back, and your grandmother will be worried sick about you.

'Could we make it in a day if we ride?' Bea asked. 'De Bois had allos at his camp.'

Theodore looked about. 'Good thinking.'

'Okay,' said Bea, 'but first we've got to say goodbye to Shola and Sheia.'

Bea and Carter ran to where Shola and Sheia were working with the other children to bring the runaway stegs together.

'I'm afraid we're going,' said Bea, embracing Sheia. 'But I'm sure we'll see one another again soon.'

'When we talked, you said you were going to have your birthday,' said Sheia.

'Yes, I did!' remembered Bea. With all that had happened, that night seemed so long ago.

'How many years will you be?' Sheia asked curiously.

'I'll be fourteen,' replied Bea.

'Same as me!' Sheia smiled. She took a colourful necklace of shells and dried nuts from around her neck, and draped it round Bea's. 'There. My present to you! From one sister to another!'

Bea looked at the necklace and her eyes filled with tears.

'Bea!' called Theodore. 'Time to go!'

Bea hugged Sheia tightly one last time. 'Yes,' she said. 'Sisters!'

28

A Grim Discovery

~ that smell again ~

It was that smell again: death. Bea, Carter, Theodore and Monty were just an hour or so away from the lodge when they caught its distinctive odour.

'This is where we were before,' said Monty. 'Where we saw the White Tyrant.'

Theodore nodded.

'I have a bad feeling about this,' he muttered, scanning the landscape.

As they drew nearer to the clearing, they heard, then saw, a swarm of insects buzzing around. Vultures and bald pteros, usually the first on the scene, were there also, squabbling over the carcass of a dead White Titan Tyrant.

'They came back, those brutes!' Bea said through gritted teeth.

Theodore dismounted and tied his allo to a fallen tree. The others did the same and joined him as he went to examine the dead Titan.

'This wasn't poachers – this is the work of a big game hunter,' said Theodore. 'Poachers are after the plates.' He pointed at the carcass. 'The tyrant's head's been cut off. It's been taken as a trophy – like the big kruger we saw. Sometimes hunters take the whole body and stuff it for display.'

Carter joined Theodore in examining the carcass. Placing a foot onto the tip of its tail, he walked the length of the tail up to its hip, and stopped. He placed the arch of one foot on the saur's hip bone, and ran the other over the top of the pelvis.

Carter had examined death many times in his life in the jungles of Aru, giving him an understanding of the anatomy of many different creatures. This Titan's ribs protruded from its chest, most likely because it had been guarding a nest and feeding a chick, giving it less time to eat, so that it had relied on a store of depleting body fat.

'There's one chick under her,' said Theodore, indicating the nest. 'The mother caught a bullet and flattened it when she fell down. She was probably trying to protect it.' He looked to the ground. 'Lots of prints – must have been a panic. There were three chicks here when we last came, almost old enough to leave the nest. They could have run.'

Carter turned away and carried on examining the dead Titan. He did not understand all these words.

Monty joined Bea, away from the smell, watching Carter stand on top of the bulk of the dead tyrant.

'Pardon me for asking, but your brother – what's his condition?'

'"His condition"?' asked Bea.

Monty looked puzzled. 'Well, he doesn't seem to be able to talk much at all. Does he have difficulty learning?'

'There's nothing wrong with him as far as we can tell, but I only met him a few months ago. We found him living in a jungle, amongst wild Raptors of Paradise,' Bea explained. 'He had been there all his life, not knowing who or what he was – he was raised as a saur.'

Monty stared at her, amazed.

'My goodness, that would make a great film! How do you know he's your brother?'

'Evidence we discovered, and it all adds up. And, more importantly, I just *know*.'

'So he's only just learning English and how to talk?'

Bea nodded.

'I guess he's going through the stages of being a child right now, discovering everything for the first time. But believe me, he's no child. He knows so much that we don't.'

Monty watched the boy with a new understanding, fascinated.

Theodore had joined Carter in carrying out an improvised autopsy on the Titan. He crouched down by its stomach, puzzled. 'The head will have made a trophy, but I'm not sure why its heart and some other organs have been removed.'

Monty walked towards the bushes to answer a call of nature, and suddenly let out a scream that had everyone running to him in alarm.

'Monty, are you all right?' asked Bea.

Monty pointed and Bea followed his finger. There was something hiding in the long grass, looking at them cautiously. She crept closer and saw it was a White Titan chick.

'It gave me a shock. But this is good, right?' asked Monty. 'It's alive.'

'Good and not so good,' muttered Theodore. 'It won't last long out here.'

'Can we take it with us?' asked Bea.

Theodore shook his head.

'It's not been done before – hand-rearing a Titan chick, that is. If we take it, then we become responsible for it. As soon as we start to feed it, we will become imprinted on it, as a parent.

Once you hand-rear or take something from the wild, it's very hard to put it back.'

Theodore couldn't help but give a rueful thought to Buster. They'd brought the Black Tyrant from its home, and it had trusted Carter, only to be set loose here to meet its fate at the hands of other predatory saurs.

'Still I dread to think how it will survive if we don't do something,' he said sadly.

Bea had been thinking too. Suddenly an idea struck her. She ran back to the nest hole, and dug out the matted lining from under the Titan's slumped body. She returned to where the others were still watching the chick. They recoiled from the way Bea stank – she was covered in the mother's blood, and other body fluids from the nest. In her arms was part of the nest. She crept downwind of the chick, and let out a cooing, calming noise. The chick sniffed the air and looked about. It was cautious at first, but gradually it let Bea inch closer. When it started to look like it was going to run off, Bea turned her back on it and sat down.

'What's she doing?' Monty whispered to Theodore, fascinated by what Bea was up to.

The chick looked at Bea with curiosity, then edged forward and nudged Bea in the back with its muzzle. She ignored it. It sniffed all around her and nudged again. Bea jabbed an elbow backwards, which made the chick back off a bit, but then it came forward again, sniffing around. Slowly, Bea pushed herself upright and walked off out of the long grass.

The chick followed.

'Let's go,' she muttered.

♦ ♦ ♦

Theodore had the task of retrieving more of the pungent nest lining, packing it into their old oil-cloth tent, and loading it onto the fourth allosaur. Then he, Carter and Monty, on their allosaurs, followed Bea and the chick at a walking pace, as Bea led them towards home.

Monty sniffed and looked at Theodore doubtfully.

'I hope you don't mind my saying so, but you stink to high heaven, old chap,' he said.

Carter nodded and held his nose to show his agreement.

'Okay,' said Theodore, shrugging. 'If you don't want my company ...'

He quickened his allo's pace, overtook Bea and the chick, and arrived at the lodge well ahead of them, in time to dig a nest hole in one of the stables and deposit his part of the original lining into it.

The smell was so pungent it reached Bunty inside the lodge, who came out to see what was going on. By the time Bea strode proudly up the drive with the Titan chick next to her, a crowd had gathered. Micki snapped away, impressed with her protégé, and even seemed glad to see that Monty had survived.

'That was smart thinking, Bea. Well done,' said Theodore. 'How did you figure out that might work?'

'I remembered when Chips, my bunny, rejected one of her kits and I had to rear it,' said Bea. 'I took some of the straw nest that had wee and poop on it, so it would feel like it was home. This seemed like the same thing.' She smiled. 'Only much smellier!'

29

The Hound of the Baskervilles

~ a cat with a half-dead mouse ~

Because of the overpowering smell, Bunty would not let them inside the lodge itself. Mo hosed down Theodore where he stood, fully clothed, boots and all, and dragged an old tin bath out for Bea to soak in, outside her room on the verandah. A hot bath, watching the sunset, was deeply satisfying after her recent ordeals. She sank into the bathwater and looked at the glorious setting sun.

The next time it rises I will be fourteen years old, she thought to herself, staring at the necklace her friend Sheia had given her.

♦ ♦ ♦

They decided that the White Tyrant chick should have very little human contact, if it were to have any chance of being released back into the wild.

'It needs to be given a wounded animal to play with, if it's to learn how to hunt,' said Theodore. 'Like a cat with a half-dead mouse. So I'm going to set some traps near the nest hole, with some snares in.'

Bea felt sorry for whatever it was that would stumble into the traps, but she knew it was the right thing to do. In the meantime, they asked the cook to chop up half a goat into manageable bits, and Carter tipped them over the stable door so the chick couldn't see it was Carter feeding it.

Lambert was concerned that the magnificent creature he'd ridden out to see only two days earlier was now dead.

'And what of the other chicks?' he asked. 'We counted three in the nest.'

'One dead, and I'm fairly sure the missing one is dead as well. That would certainly have been the fate of the one Monty found, if Bea hadn't saved it.'

After dinner, they all watched as Monty acted out the part of the adventure when the three of them had arrived in Micki's plane. Lambert and Micki particularly chuckled at Monty's exaggerated actions, and everyone oohed and aahed as if they were watching Monty's latest picture. It was obvious Micki was impressed with Monty. Gone were the cutting remarks she had previously used to put him down.

Bunty was very pleased with the news that Michael Keat was safe and well, and smiled broadly when Theodore said that Keat had suggested joining their two estates together, now he'd recovered his from De Bois's clutches.

'That's a wonderful idea,' Bunty said, 'but what if we handed the land back to the Steggi? If you think about it, asking them to work for us, looking out for poachers and whatnot – in return for the privilege of living on the land they rightfully own – well, we would be just as bad as De Bois.'

Theodore nodded. Bunty was right and he knew it.

'That's a great idea!' said Micki. 'I've something to add too. How about we reshoot the article about Monty, and write in this new twist? I have lots of footage I can use. '

'Yes!' enthused Monty. 'The angle at the moment is all wrong. We need to be promoting what this reserve stands for. Preserving the wildlife and the landscape, rather than killing and exploiting it.'

Micki clapped her hands in approval.

'Let's go back to what's left of the Titan nest and photograph the dead body; shock people, tell them the truth about this barbaric sport and the hurt it causes. We can call it "Hunting the Hunters"!' She turned to Bea. 'We'll need a photo of you and Monty with the Titan chick you saved.'

As Bea blushed, Monty grinned and said to his publicist: 'That's your cover shot, right there!'

◆ ◆ ◆

Eventually everyone departed to their rooms, high in spirits from the stories, revelations and new plans, leaving Theodore with Monty and a bottle of brandy.

'Thank you,' said Theodore. 'It's quite a thing you're doing to help here.'

'No, thank you!' Monty returned the compliment.

'What for?' asked Theodore. 'I almost got you killed several times!'

'For showing me how to be a real hero.'

Theodore raised his eyebrow and Monty copied as they clinked glasses and swigged back the brandy.

'I've got a feeling I'll be playing you in the film!' said Monty, causing Theodore to spurt his mouthful into the fire, causing a mini fireball.

Just as they were considering opening the second bottle, Mo ran in, looking worried.

'I was closing up the stables. Something is up with the Titan chick; it's making strange noises. Could you come, Theodore?'

'Allow me to undertake this mission, Watson!' said Monty in an English accent, as he got to his feet.

Mo and Theodore looked at him, puzzled.

'*Hound of the Baskervilles*,' added Monty. 'My next movie. I'm playing Sherlock Holmes. I need to practise.'

'Okay,' said Theodore. 'You can come too. But Mo's in charge here.'

Theodore got his pistol, and they headed for the stables. Fortunately, the moon was high and lit the path ahead.

Suddenly they heard a strange whimpering sound.

Monty stopped.

'It's wounded, I tell you,' he said. 'Ready your firearm, Watson, we can't take any chances.'

Theodore chuckled. They had drunk quite a lot and the bizarreness of the situation had overtaken him.

'Careful with that, Watson,' said Monty. He pointed to the revolver in Theodore's hand. 'Or I'll have Lestrade arrest you and throw you in the clink for being drunk in charge of a deadly weapon!'

As they both burst into laughter, they heard the groaning again, and stopped, suddenly alert.

'The door of the stable is open,' said Mo urgently. 'Something else is inside!'

The three men pushed into the stable.

A semi-conscious man was slumped in the nest hole that Theodore had dug. He was groaning and feebly pushing the tyrant chick away, as it happily nipped at him, pulling away the man's clothes as if they were flesh.

'Good Lord!' said Monty, stunned.

'He must have slipped on a chunk of goat in the darkness,' said Theodore, 'and fallen into the nesting hole.'

Theodore pulled the groaning man safely out of the stable by his feet. Mo shut the stable door before shining the torch on the man's face to see who it was.

Theodore immediately pulled the man up by the scruff of his neck and knocked him out cold with one punch.

'Good heavens, what's got into you?' burst out Monty.

Theodore turned the man over and pushed his face

into the dirt, as he looped some rope around his wrists.

He turned to Monty.

'I should have left him in there to be eaten alive. He's the one you want to lock up!'

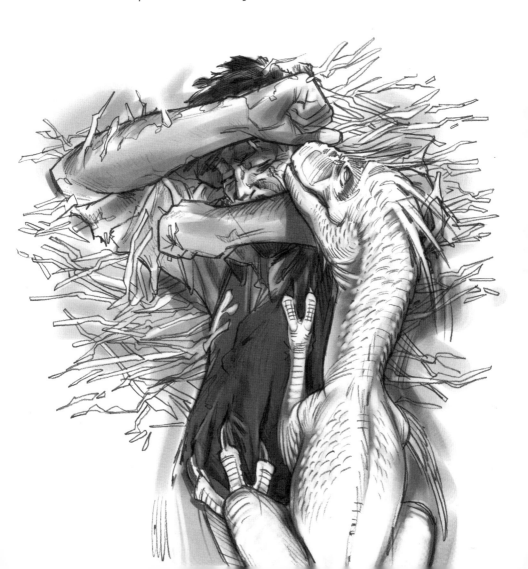

30

Christian Hayter

~ that horrid little man ~

'Christian Hayter, that horrid little man!' Bunty stared at Theodore and Monty, shocked. 'How on earth did he wind up in the stables?'

'Your guess is as good as mine.' Theodore shrugged. 'I thought he'd been buried by the cave explosion.'

'Good morning,' said Lambert, coming down for breakfast. 'Spot of bother?'

'Definitely,' Bunty barked.

'We had a prowler here last night. Someone known to us,' said Theodore.

'Well, I hope you booted him off your land.'

'No. He's locked up in the basement.'

Lambert frowned.

'Why, what did he do?'

'He was in the nest with the White Tyrant chick. He'd fallen in.'

Lambert looked doubtful.

'It seems a bit extreme,' he said. 'I mean, you can't go around locking people up for falling in holes.'

'Believe me, whatever Christian Hayter was up to, it's worthy of being locked up,' said Theodore darkly.

'Hayter!' exclaimed Bea, who'd joined them. 'Here?'

Theodore nodded.

'Monty, Mo and I caught him last night, in the stables.'

'But I thought he died at the caves!'

Lambert looked at them, intrigued.

'Christian Hayter,' he murmured. 'Should I know the name?'

Bunty looked at Theodore, who gave a brief shake of his head out of Lambert's eyeline.

'No,' she said to her guest. 'He's just a lowlife we bumped into during our travels.'

♦ ♦ ♦

Theodore left them discussing the events of the night before, Monty once again giving them his own version, this time as Holmes saving the intruder from the Hound of the Baskervilles. He went down to the basement, where Hayter was slumped on a wooden chair, tied up with stout ropes. Hayter looked up as Theodore entered.

'I smell coffee,' he said.

'I thought you'd died with De Bois,' said Theodore.

Hayter grinned. 'I took shelter from the stegs as they ran. Lucky decision on my part.'

'Why are you here?'

'How about some coffee before questions?' said Hayter.

'You'll get coffee if you tell me the truth.'

Hayter smirked.

'Okay. I've been following you. I followed you all the way from Aru. Now, can I have three sugars?'

Theodore stepped forward, his fists clenched threateningly.

'Why have you been following us?'

'You stole my Beast from me. Where is it, by the way? I didn't see it in the stable.'

'You didn't follow us all this way just because of the tyrant. Tell me something I can believe.'

Hayter still wore his smirk. 'You're slightly balding. Sorry, you must know that already.'

Theodore didn't respond, just kept his angry glare fixed on Hayter. Hayter kept grinning.

'All right then, how about I tell you this? When I get out of here I'm going to kill you. Sorry, my mistake. You must know that as well.'

Theodore, filled with rage, swung a punch towards Hayter's face, but stopped just before he hit him. Hayter, however, had shunted back, losing balance, and he and the chair fell to the floor. He looked up at Theodore and gave another mocking smirk.

'So, three sugars?'

♦ ♦ ♦

As Theodore came out of the basement, he met Lambert at the top of the stairs.

'Has your prisoner said anything?' the older man asked.

Theodore shook his head, still angry and not trusting himself to speak.

'Do you think he was the hunter who killed the female Titan?' Lambert pondered.

'Not possible,' said Theodore shortly. 'He couldn't have done it alone.'

'Has he said who his accomplices were?'

Again, Theodore shook his head.

'Not a word. Just a cruel smirk that tells me he's up to his ears in something big.'

He and Lambert returned to the breakfast room, where Bunty shot him an enquiring look.

'Nothing,' grunted Theodore. 'He's staying silent.'

'It might be better to let the authorities deal with it,' said Lambert. 'My servants aren't doing much here, just freeloading and having a holiday. How about we let them do some proper work and escort your fugitive, this Hayter chap, over to Ranj in Nairobi? He can get the authorities to deal with him properly.'

Bunty sighed.

'Thank you, Lambert, but what are we actually charging him with? Trespassing amounts to a minor incident. We need to find out more. Until we can pin evidence on Hayter, that he was hunting without a permit and was responsible for killing the Titan, the only thing we can do is let him go.'

'Not yet!' said Theodore.

'But we have no evidence against him,' said Bunty. 'I loathe him as much as you do, Theodore, but …'

'I'll get the evidence,' insisted Theodore.

'A confession that's beaten out of someone won't stand up in court,' said Lambert. He looked at Bunty apologetically. 'I'm sorry to throw a spanner in the works.'

'No, Lambert, you're quite right,' said Bunty with a sigh. She looked at Theodore. 'Sadly, we really have to let him go.'

'No!' repeated Theodore, forcefully this time. 'I know Hayter's type. I'll get what I want from him. Give me more time. He's vain. He'll want to boast of how clever he is – I can see it in his eyes, in the smug way he looks at me. He will tell me what's really going on and who his accomplices are. Then we'll take him to the authorities.'

Bunty looked at Theodore.

'Okay,' she sighed. 'But tomorrow we must decide what to do. We can't keep him locked up for ever, Theodore.'

'Well, if there's anything I can do …' offered Lambert. He went to Bunty and gently took her hands in his. 'I want you to feel that you can ask me anything.'

'Thank you, Lambert. That is a great comfort.'

He bowed and kissed her hands, then smiled gently at both her and Theodore as he left the room.

'Did you ever see such a charming man?' sighed Bunty.

'He's smooth, certainly,' said Theodore grudgingly. He looked around the breakfast room. 'Where's Bea?'

'She went to her room,' answered Bunty. 'Why?'

Theodore gestured at the calendar on the wall.

'With all that's been happening, I bet she thinks we've forgotten. Certainly, I've been too occupied with that rat, Hayter …'

Bunty put her hand to her mouth, aghast.

'Bea's birthday!' she gasped.

✦ ✦ ✦

Bea was sat on her bed. She felt so miserable. Today, which should have been so special, was just ... dreadful.

She'd been excited to come downstairs when she woke up. But they'd all forgotten. Bunty and Theodore, her own family. Despite her intention not to let it get to her, she felt tears well up in her eyes and roll down her cheeks, and suddenly she was crying, great sobs of misery.

There was a knock on her door, and hastily she tried to gather herself together, picking up a pillow to bury her face in and wipe her eyes.

'One moment ...'

'Oh, my poor, dear darling girl!' Bunty was already in the room. She plonked herself down on the bed next to Bea and threw her arms around her granddaughter. 'What must you think of us! But it's been such a dreadful time, with Hayter turning up, and the hunters and the abandoned chick ...' Bunty hugged Bea tightly. 'But, Happy Birthday, my darling. Now, dry your eyes. Everybody's waiting for you downstairs.'

✦ ✦ ✦

And everybody was. Theodore was smiling, holding a parcel that was so badly wrapped it looked as if it might come open at any moment. Lambert, along with Monty, Micki and Carter, applauded and cheered, and sang 'Happy Birthday' as Bea walked into the reception room with Bunty. It was obvious that Carter had no real idea of what was going on, but he knew something nice was happening for his sister, and he joined in as loudly as anyone.

He's never known a birthday, Bea realised. And she ran over and hugged him tightly, and the tears that ran down her cheeks this time were tears of happiness.

'We've got a birthday treat lined up for you,' said Monty.

'The reshoot we were talking about,' said Micki. 'As well as the photo of you and Monty with the Titan chick you saved, we'd like you and Carter to come out with us and finish of the rest of the shoot. Tell us how it should be done and be photographed by the nest.'

'And when you return, we've planned a special birthday dinner in your honour,' said Bunty.

'To which your grandmother has kindly invited me,' said Lambert. He smiled. 'I think that's so that it will be harder for you to refuse.'

'What's to refuse?' burst out Bea delightedly.

Me, going on a shoot with a Hollywood movie star, one of the world's greatest photographers and my new-found long-lost brother, with a special dinner to follow, she thought. *This is the greatest birthday ever!*

31

Fate's Lucky Cards

~ *the godfather* ~

The reshoot went well. Carter and the game warden kept lookout in case the male tyrant returned. When they arrived, a pack of hyenas were getting stuck into the dead tyrant. Carter let out some very convincing Ronax barks that made them scatter, but they hung around for a while and only moved on when a Thinhorn Tritops wandered past.

As Micki took her shots of the dead Titan, she found her appreciation and respect growing towards the man she had once mocked, as Monty shed some genuine tears. He was off camera, and being himself. His once pristine clothes were now tattered and torn from his adventures, and he had waved away his stylist, who wanted to sew them up.

Once the shots were taken, they returned to the lodge. After a hearty lunch, Micki set Bea up for her cover shoot by the stables with the Titan chick, and because the light was perfect, everyone gathered for a final group photo.

Then it was time for Micki
and Monty, along with his entourage, to pack
for their respective journeys home. Monty had his people
to do his packing for him, so he thought he'd be ready first,
but when he walked into the lounge, Micki was already
standing there in her flying jacket, her helmet in one hand.

Monty smiled. 'Going somewhere?'

She smiled back at him and murmured seductively:
'What if I was?'

Monty swept in, took her gloved hand, swung her

round, and pulled her in close till their lips almost touched.

'I would hunt you down and make you pay for breaking my heart.'

Micki blushed.

'Well, I am heading off to Nairobi then Mombasa – via a few desolate and inhospitable pitstops – in an hour. Is that enough time for you to hunt me down?'

Monty looked past her at his agent, who'd just walked in, and waved him away. The agent hesitated, then made a swift exit.

'It may take longer than that,' whispered Monty. 'Is there room for one more in the *Dragonfly*?'

Micki pulled him closer to her, and kissed him.

'Does that answer your question?'

♦ ♦ ♦

A leaving party gathered to wave them both off. Monty took a light bag with him and made arrangements with his agent to meet up in Mombasa. He signed pictures of himself that Micki had developed for the staff, and promised them all a credit in his next film. It was obvious from the worried looks on the faces of his entourage that they were concerned; Monty had never been away without at least three people to do things for him. It was also possible this sudden freedom might mean their future employment was coming to an end.

As they headed towards the plane, Carter hissed at Monty and pretended to try to bite to him, to which Monty replied with an equally chilling White Tyrant roar,

and bobbed about, sizing up his shadow raptor opponent. They paraded about, scuffing the ground and intimidating each other, but as Monty lunged in a tyrant attack, he gave the boy a big hug.

'Keep acting, kid! You're a star!'

Bea got a kiss on both cheeks from him.

'You and me, kid, saving the saurs!' He handed her something soft wrapped up in tissue paper. 'I wanted to give you something for your birthday, and my stylist suggested this would be appropriate. I believe they're all the rage now.' He blushed a little as he explained, 'My stylist packs for all occasions and events, including... gifts for ladies.' He was clearly somewhat embarrassed at his old self.

Bea opened the present to find a wonderful new, short dress that was much more fitted and in fashion than the dresses Bunty had packed for her.

Micki dipped into her flying jacket and handed Bea a pocket camera.

'Here, a birthday present from me. I started out with this, and I expect you to use it well, young lady.'

Bea was overcome. A camera! It was the best present she could have wished for.

'Oh, I will!' she promised.

'Good. I look forward to seeing your shots in print one day.'

Monty jogged over to Theodore to shake his hand, then they saluted one other.

Micki climbed into the pilot's seat, and Monty sat behind. In no time at all, everyone was looking up at the plane in the sky. A loop-the-loop later, and the *Dragonfly* was out of sight.

◆ ◆ ◆

That evening it seemed very quiet at the lodge. Everyone made an effort to dress up for Bea's birthday dinner, with Carter putting on his smart matching jacket and shorts. He couldn't be persuaded to wear the shoes again, however.

'Beatrice Brownlee, if I had known I was visiting on your birthday, I would have brought something with me.' Lambert smiled as Bea swirled in her new dress to show off its modern hemline and satin neck-bow.

'Lambert, it's fine. I'm just happy to be here and not in a cave! And please, it's Bea to friends. Bea Kingsley.'

Lambert frowned.

'Kingsley? Not Brownlee, like your grandmother?'

'Brownlee is my mother's maiden name. My father was Franklin Kingsley.'

Lambert suddenly spluttered, choking on his drink. Bea looked at him in consternation.

'My apologies,' Lambert said, composing himself. 'Please excuse me, Barbara, but was your daughter called Grace, by any chance?'

Stunned into silence, Bunty looked at Theodore and Bea. It was Carter who spoke, having picked up the sudden change in the room.

'My mother name?'

Lambert looked at Carter, stunned.

'Your mother?' Then he shook his head, a troubled expression on his face. 'If what I think is true, then this may be not the right time to discuss it,' he said.

'On the contrary,' said Theodore. 'I think we all want to know how you knew Grace and Franklin.'

Lambert looked around at them, as if he was trying to find the words. Then he looked to Carter and said: 'You are Carter Kingsley?'

Carter nodded.

'How can this be so?' Lambert shook his head. 'I thought you were dead! Who found you?'

'We did,' said Bunty.

'Where? How? On Aru?'

Bunty and Theodore exchanged quizzical looks, then Bunty said: 'Yes, on Aru. We've just come from there.'

'I thought you said he lived in Australia?'

'Sorry, Lambert,' said Theodore. 'It seemed an easier explanation for strangers than the truth. We actually found him living with the shadow raptors on Aru. He was raised by them. But how do you know about Carter?'

'Yes, please,' urged Bunty. 'Tell us what you know of Grace and Franklin, and how you knew about Carter.'

Lambert looked at them, hesitating, and obviously struggling with his words.

'You don't know, do you?' he said. 'I'm so, so sorry.'

'What?' Bea begged him. 'Know what?'

'I was there when they all died.' He pointed at Carter. 'Including you, or so I thought. How were you spared?'

They stared at Lambert, struggling to cope with the enormity of what he was saying, as he turned to Bea and Carter.

'I met your father the evening you were born, Carter, on Aru. There was a bar in Koto Baru. It looked like Frank needed a drink, and as there were no other westerners in there, we got chatting. He wanted to celebrate the birth of his son. You're named after Howard Carter, the famous explorer, did you know that?'

They watched Lambert, hypnotised, as he elaborated the story. 'My shipping company had me there longer than I wanted to be, and so I became a familiar face. Gracie was a lovely woman. Now I know why you have a familiar smile – it's your mother's, Bea.'

Bea welled up with tears.

He turned to Carter. 'They made me your godfather.'

'Godfather?' repeated Carter, puzzled.

'It meant I was supposed to look after you, if anything happened to them. Not that we expected anything to, of course. We were all booked on the same boat home, but Frank insisted on looking for a temple of some sort.'

'A temple? Not the Raptors of Paradise?' asked Theodore.

Lambert shook his head.

'Other people would visit Aru to see the raptors, but Frank was after something more. I remember him trying to explain his research into the saurpeople.'

'Saurmen,' Theodore corrected him.

'That's it! Saurmen. I still have a journal of his, you know.' Lambert fitted the parts of his memory together as he looked at Theodore. 'In fact, Frank mentions you in his writing, something about how he and Theo found the twins?'

Theodore gulped and looked around the room. Everyone's attention had turned from Lambert to Theodore.

'The twins,' Theodore repeated. 'What else did he mention?'

But Lambert shrugged a little. 'I can't recall, but it's all in the journal.'

He looked at Bea. 'Next time we meet, I'll let you have it. Your father was convinced there was a sacred temple on Aru and he knew how to find it, even though he didn't have a map or anything. Of course, your mother being the keen naturalist, she wanted to see the raptors. It was their last chance to go, and they persuaded me to accompany them.' He shook his head sadly. 'I wish I could go back in time and tell them not to.'

'We were told they were attacked,' said Bunty.

Lambert nodded. 'The raptors we saw were not pretty – far from it. Drab, large and, like they tell you in the old stories, vicious.'

Theodore saw that Carter's eyes were filling with tears, and he murmured: 'Careful, Lambert. He's only eleven, and still trying to understand things. You're talking about the family who raised him.'

'He needs to know the truth,' Lambert said. 'You all need to know the truth! Those monsters came out of the shadows.' He looked directly at Carter and said: 'The raptors tore your mother in two and ripped you away from her dying arms. Frank fought like mad but was taken down. I got this.' Lambert pointed to the deep scar on his cheek.

'I played dead, then crept off when it all went quiet. It took me four days to find my way out of the jungle. I was delirious with fever by the time I made it back to Koto Baru.'

Lambert stood up and walked over to Carter, placing a hand on his shoulder. 'I deserted you, my godson, when you were a vulnerable baby boy. Your father entrusted me, a relative stranger, with an honourable task, and I failed. I truly believed you were dead. Then, out of the blue, eleven years later I am saved from being savaged by a tyrant by the same boy. Fate has dealt us lucky cards, my boy. I am for ever in your debt and so, so sorry. Please forgive me.'

◆ ◆ ◆

After dinner, Bea felt exhausted. She had wished on every previous birthday that her parents were there to share it. She had wished she knew where they were, wished she knew why they were not there with her. Now, on her fourteenth birthday, she finally knew the whole truth.

While Bunty, Theodore and Lambert talked it over and over, Bea joined her brother under the table.

Carter was contemplating shoes. He was comparing the differences in style, colour and shape between the two men's: Lambert's sharp, shiny shoes, with a raised heel, and Theodore's older lace-ups. Bea took her necklace off, opened up the silver locket and looked at the pictures of her parents.

'I didn't know them, and neither did you.' She pointed upwards, to the table above them where the adults were reminiscing about Grace and Kingsley. 'They did. Sadly, we can never be part of these conversations.'

She handed the locket to her brother. Carter placed his finger and thumb over each face. They were just as small as the first time he had seen them, but now he knew how their faces had got there. Photographed and developed in dark room bathed in a magical liquid.

32

The Swarm

~ one in a million, million ~

The next morning, Bunty pulled Theodore to one side after breakfast.

'I have known you long enough to tell when something is up, Theodore. You've been distracted ever since Lambert mentioned Franklin's journal. Tell me, who are these twins?' She gave him a sharp look. 'You skirted around that as if you had no idea what he was talking about, but you do, don't you?'

Theodore knew not to deny Bunty the truth, but now was not the right time for it.

'Can I answer when I've learned a little more of this journal Lambert has?' he said instead. 'It relates to something from back home.'

'What's in England that's such a secret?' Bunty asked, puzzled.

'Not England. Our old home, in California – the Kingsley ranch. It's Franklin's secret, not mine. I've never told a soul … and I'm not entirely sure whether I should now, in the light of what happened.'

Bunty glared at him, frustrated. 'The journal Lambert has must be a companion to the one we found in Franklin's trunk on Aru.' Theodore nodded as Bunty continued pointedly, 'Have you read it, Theodore? What's in it?'

'Nothing much,' Theodore replied evasively. 'Random notes, some research into … strange things, curiosities and folklore. Don't tell Lambert we have it yet,' he added quickly.

Bunty had more questions, but Lambert was outside the breakfast room and she could see now was not the time.

'I want to read the journal we have,' she said forcefully. 'Bring it to my room after dinner.'

Theodore nodded wearily. The events of his past were

catching up with him. He was reluctantly coming to the conclusion that eventually Bunty would find out that he knew a lot more than he was letting on.

The rest of the day was subdued. Lambert was morose, and had outbursts of guilt – that everything would have been different, if only he'd stopped Franklin and Grace going into the rainforest. Bunty did her best to reassure him it wasn't his fault. She told him that Grace's curiosity was only matched by Franklin's.

'You could never have persuaded them not to go,' she told him. 'You weren't to blame in any way. And now … you've found Carter again. And you've found us.'

But Lambert's feelings of guilt were soon of secondary importance. It was Carter who noticed the swarm first.

He saw a big, fat locust land on his arm. It was a lot bigger than the types back home on Aru, and he was very happy to see it. This looked very tasty indeed. He grabbed it in his hand and bit its head clean off. It tasted good.

To his joy, another landed next to him. He swiped it up, removed the wings, and ate it whole. He closed his eyes and for a moment was back home, amongst the clan of shadow raptors. Then a scream split the air.

He opened his eyes to see that the sky had darkened because of a huge cloud that was racing towards the lodge. Mo burst from the garage with a big red barrel under his arm, and proceeded to pour liquid onto piles of grass that were dotted all along the perimeter of the lodge grounds. Another man started closing up the doors and lowering the hatches. Staff in the house busied themselves closing all the windows from inside. The groundskeeper ran around and unlatched all the open shutters and bolted them shut.

Theodore appeared and shouted: 'We have to be quick! Carter, come with me!'

'What happen?' asked Carter.

'Locusts. Got to keep them from settling.' He gestured wildly with his arms to make sure Carter understood. 'If we don't, they will strip everything before moving on.'

Theodore and Carter helped light the small fires one by one. However, to the east of the lodge there were no prepared fires. Theodore saw a suitably dry bush and lit it with a flaming torch, while Mo splashed a large puddle of kerosene onto the lawn and darted away before Theodore tossed a match onto it. The fires all around the grounds created thick smoke – it was a desperate bid to deter the ravenous swarm.

A locust flew past one of the fires at the exact moment a spark from it flew into the air. This spark had a one-in-a-million chance of hitting the locust mid-flight. The locust – swerving around and on fire, like a shot-down fighter plane – had a one in a million, million chance of flying through a crack in an open window as it was being closed.

And that is how the fire started: a flaming locust crawling down the net curtains.

A servant's shout of alarm brought Lambert running into the living room, where he saw that the fire was spreading rapidly. Already the armchairs by the window were ablaze. He grabbed a vase of flowers and hurled them and the water at the flames, but they had no effect.

Then he heard a thudding noise coming from somewhere below, and shouting from someone in distress.

Smoke was filling the room and spreading into the house. Lambert put his handkerchief to his nose and mouth, and made his way downstairs to the basement.

'Help!' yelled Hayter. 'Someone let me out! It's filling with smoke down here!'

Lambert tried the handle, but the door was locked.

'Is someone down there?'

It was Bunty calling.

'We need help!' shouted Lambert.

Bunty appeared through the smoke.

'Do you have a key?' he shouted. 'The prowler is locked in here! We have to get him out!'

Bunty fumbled with a bunch of keys, selected one and held it out to him.

'Here, you do it, I'm all fingers and thumbs,' she said.

Lambert turned it in the lock, and the door swung wide, belching the smoke outwards. Christian Hayter fell at Lambert's feet.

'Thank you, boss!' He coughed with relief. 'I knew you'd come back for me!'

Bunty looked to Lambert.

'What did he call you?' she asked.

Too late, Christian Hayter saw Bunty behind Lambert Knútr.

'You fool!' Lambert growled at Hayter. 'I've told you before, never to call me boss!'

Lambert Knútr grabbed Bunty by the arm and thrust her into the smoke-filled room, then locked the door.

'Lambert! What are you doing?!' called Bunty, desperately banging on the locked door.

'I'm "the Viscount" to you, got it?' Lambert yelled at Hayter, and with that he hurried to the stairs. Hayter followed, both men battling their way through the thick smoke as Bunty's cries followed them: 'Let me out! Let me out!!!'

♦ ♦ ♦

Outside, Bea was with Mo, each of them waving a smouldering branch to ward off the locusts, when suddenly she saw the flames leaping out from the roof of the lodge.

'Mo!' she screamed. 'The lodge! It's on fire!'

Immediately she and Mo began checking who was there and who wasn't. She saw Theodore, Carter, Lambert, the servants …

'Where's Bunty?' she shouted.

'She was inside!' Mo yelled back.

He threw his branch down and ran towards the lodge, Bea following and shouting for help. Carter and

Theodore both heard Bea's panicky shout and rushed to the house.

'The door's jammed!' shouted Mo.

'We think Bunty's inside!' wailed Bea.

Theodore hurled himself at the locked front door and took out both the door and frame in one hit. The flames inside blew out, but as fresh oxygen was sucked in through the gaping hole, the fire burst into renewed life.

The fire now raged out of control – glass and windows were shattering under the intense heat as parts of the building began to collapse from within. Theodore ran through the flames and disappeared into the house. Bea went to run after him, but Carter stopped her, pulling her away just as the door lintel gave way and the porch crashed to the ground.

Lambert appeared, pushing them aside, and ran into the burning house, reappearing a few moments later, supporting the barely conscious Theodore. They crashed to the ground.

Bea ran to Lambert. 'Bunty?' she begged.

Lambert looked at her, then shook his head.

33

After the Fire

~ everything tastes foul ~

Dawn brought the news everyone had dreaded, but hoped would not be true.

'We found her in the basement,' said Mo. 'It looks as if the door was locked.'

'With Hayter?' Theodore asked.

Mo shook his head.

'We only found one body. It's definitely her. The smoke was too much for her. Barbara must have tried to free Hayter, and he repaid her by locking her in there.'

Tears sprang into Theodore's eyes.

'That man will pay for this!' he vowed.

Bea and Carter sat in the stables in silence, feeling numbed. They had watched Mo's men pulling the smouldering wreckage of the lodge apart, trying to save what they could. A scorched chair, a cracked vase and a blackened picture frame started the collection of salvageable items on the driveway.

Lambert appeared from the servants' quarters, close to where Mo lived, holding a pot of coffee and two empty tin cups. He offered one of the cups of Theodore.

'Try some of this,' he said.

Theodore took one of the cups and Lambert poured the coffee for them.

'How are you doing?' Lambert asked, his voice filled with sympathy.

'I'm thinking of what I'll do to Hayter when I find him,' muttered Theodore darkly. 'Did anyone see him?'

Lambert shook his head.

'Everyone inside was concentrating on fighting the fire.'

They sipped at the coffee. Theodore scowled and emptied his cup on the ground.

'Sorry about that; it's stewed and barely warm, but all I could find,' Lambert apologised.

'It's not that,' said Theodore. 'It's just … thinking of Bunty trapped in that room … What sort of man could do that to her?' He shook his head. 'Everything tastes foul at the moment.' He forced a smile. 'I never got to thank you for running in after me, Lambert. I owe you one. A big one.'

'You would have done the same – think nothing of it,' said Lambert with a shrug. 'I was talking to Mo. He tells me he has all the paperwork in his office about the estate. Keat's as well as Bunty's. Shall I drop them off with Ranj, to keep everything safe? One less job for you to do. After all, I'm returning the car and servants to the polo club.'

Theodore nodded. 'That rat Christian Hayter! Why was he following us? He had so many chances to kill us, but he didn't. There was something to gain by just keeping tabs on us – but what?'

'Perhaps one day you'll find the answer,' said Lambert. He walked over to where Bea and Carter were sitting.

'It's a sad time, and I know it's a cruel destiny that has brought us all together, but I am so glad to be reacquainted with you, Carter, after all these years. And you, Beatrice. You've both lost so much in your short lives. Your parents, and now your grandmother. The only light is that you have found each other, and I have found my godson again. I have no children, and no one to pass my knowledge and wealth on to. I failed in protecting you, Carter, and it caused me pain that I've carried ever since, until just two days ago. Now fate has given me a second chance to redeem myself and fill the role I was given. I would like to also extend that to you, Beatrice. Please, consider me godfather to you both.'

Her eyes filled with tears, Bea got to her feet and went to Lambert and hugged him tightly. Carter, too, rose and embraced him.

'Carter, Beatrice – anything you need, anything, please ask,' said Lambert. 'I am family now.'

34

The Funeral

~ the purpose of holes ~

Over the following week, the lodge started to spring back to life. The burnt remains were cleared and the scorched patches dotted around the grounds were turning green again, with yellow flowers appearing. Builders had already constructed a basic wooden frame over the old plot, and under Mo's direction the new lodge was taking shape.

Mr Keat was as good as his word. Ranjit organised the best lawyers and solicitors to sort out the mess De Bois had caused, and plans were drawn up to join the two estates together. In addition to this, everyone agreed that the land should be handed over to its rightful owners, the Steggi, just as Bunty had wished. The lodge would pay rent to them for the land it used as the reserve and for permits to watch and observe the wildlife that they would all look after. Somehow another diamond turned up to pay for everything, and Michael Keat had a very good idea where some more might be in case funds were needed in the future.

Word of Bunty's tragic death stretched all the way over to Nairobi and as far as Mombasa, prompting Monty and Micki to fly back and pay their respects. The sky was filled as people flew in from all directions.

Everyone turned out for the funeral, including an almost unrecognisable Michael Keat, clean-shaven in a suit. Bea had picked some spindly yellow flowers for them all to hold, and Theodore gave a moving elegy. Carter managed to wear shoes, and Bea bravely held back her tears as everyone said a little something about the great woman, who would be missed by all. Bunty was finally laid to rest next to Sidney so they could look out over the epic view together for ever.

One by one the funeral party paid their last respects, and made their way back home. Ranjit helped Mo clear up, giving Theodore, Bea and Carter some private space to linger by Bunty's and Sidney's graves.

Carter had not yet cried. His emotions were not tuned in like the others. He felt the same loss, but did not know how to release it. Somehow he felt that the terrible events were caused by him. That if he hadn't left the island of Aru to become human, Bunty would still be alive.

Suddenly, as this feeling came over him, a tear dropped from his eye and onto his grandmother's grave. Bea watched as her brother suddenly sank to the ground, sobbing. Theodore patted him on the back.

'Let it out, lad. Let it out.'

Carter's sobbing grew louder, and then suddenly his sorrow turned to anger. What little he knew of the human world was filled with pain, suffering and death. The saurs he knew only killed to survive. Humans, it seemed, killed for everything else: greed, money, hatred and sport.

Carter clenched the freshly turned soil in his hands and screamed at the world. He screamed and screamed so loudly that birds lifted from the nearby trees. Then he slumped onto the grave, his body shaking with uncontrollable sobs.

Bea, unable to watch her brother in so much pain, had turned away helplessly. So she was the first to see the dust cloud emerging over a ridge on the horizon. Apprehensively, she nudged Theodore and pointed, muttering 'Locusts' nervously.

'No,' muttered back Theodore. 'Locusts blacken the view, not stir up dust. The dust has been stirred up by something else.'

Everyone's eyes were now on the huge approaching cloud, which was coming towards them like a fog over the land. Carter was still crouched on the ground, consumed by grief.

To the north, a similar cloud was stirring across the grassy plains, and to the east, smaller swirls of dirt sent birds aloft. Like some magical tornado, the blankets of dust collected and swirled all around the old lodge, and the ground beneath their feet began to shake.

'Is it an earthquake?' asked Bea, worried.

The ground suddenly stopped shaking, and the loose leaves and dirt started to swirl gently and very slowly downwards to the ground. Whatever had been causing the dust cloud had stopped moving. As the dust began to settle, the thin shape of a tall man holding a long spear slowly appeared, and he walked up to them. It was the stegosorcerer.

'It has become clear who the message is for,' he told them calmly.

As the dust cloud vanished, other shapes to appear. The unmistakable silhouette of a majestic stegosaur was the first one Bea could make out. Behind it, something much larger stood and dipped its head forward – an African brachio. Theodore spun around. Out of the dust loomed many different saurs. They had been travelling at speed and caused the dust cloud.

Several types of tritops appeared. Beside them the smaller krugers stood beside each other. A pack of wild phalox pushed their way to the front, with their domed bony heads.

'How did you gather all the saurs here?' Theodore asked the stegosorcerer.

'I did not do this.' He pointed his staff at Carter, curled up on the ground. 'He called to them and they heard his pain.'

Bea nudged her brother. 'Carter. Get up!'

Carter slowly heard his sister calling, and felt her shaking him back to reality from the dark place into which he had slipped. Then he heard another voice he knew, and blinked his red eyes open. He spun his head each way, and picked himself up to face hundreds of eyes looking intently at him. Saurs of every shape and colour, many of which he had never seen before, surrounded them in silence.

'They have come to meet you,' said the stegosorcerer.

Suddenly a horned tyrant appeared, swinging its strong head around and facing them all.

Theodore looked at the hundreds of varieties of saurs around them. A fearful realisation suddenly struck him.

'Carnivores on one side, and herbivores on the other,' he murmured apprehensively to Bea. 'And us right in the middle. This is big trouble. We could be in the eye of a very big storm.'

Carter rose to his feet as the tyrant came in closer and gave Carter a good sniff. Then they heard a high-pitched barking from behind them. Theodore looked with concern towards the noise.

'Ronax. Please, not a Ronax!' he murmured, quietly pleading.

Like an echo, another similar bark replied from the other side, then a few more joined in from the left and right.

'Great, we're surrounded by a pack of Ronax,' Theodore said. 'This can't get any worse.'

Carter, however, seemed somehow unfazed, as one by one the Ronax crept in, snipping at other saurs to get out of the way and barking signals to the others. The Lonesome Horned Tyrant opened its mouth wide and repeatedly tutted its tongue on the roof of its mouth. The sound was like someone drumming their fingers loudly, waiting for something to happen.

'It's a warning sound, like a rattlesnake. This is not good, Bea. We've got to run,' said Theodore urgently.

'Where to?' asked Bea. 'We're surrounded!'

She looked at her brother, who was watching the mass of saurs with almost an air of serenity. She looked at the stegosorcerer, who had his eyes shut tightly and was muttering to himself. One Ronax popped its head out between two styracos that were shaking with nerves, and was spotted by the now not-so-Lonesome Horned Tyrant, who turned to tut directly at it.

'I promise you, Bea, it's about to kick off here, big time,' said Theodore, worried. 'Let's get out of here.'

'No,' Bea said, watching her brother. 'Trust Carter. This is happening, Theodore. Pull yourself together.'

'Okay, stay calm, stay calm,' Theodore muttered under his breath.

'I am calm,' Bea replied.

'I'm talking to myself,' he said.

Bea turned slowly. The horned tyrant kept tutting and was now shifting his eyes about, trying to keep track of the Ronax. The front line of herbivores looked like they were ready to bolt in all directions under the tension, and even though the herbivores were not going to eat them, they had horns, spikes and plates, and massive bulks that would flatten or impale humans in a moment.

Something nudged her from behind and Bea yelped. The White Tyrant chick had somehow found its way out of the stable, and was curious to get into the middle of things. It slipped up to Bea and squawked.

Something at the back of the mass of saurs heard the vulnerable chick and growled out a long low roar, which made all the other saurs even more twitchy. The Ronax immediately stopped barking and the horned tyrant stopped tutting, closed its mouth and stood tall, ready to face whatever had roared. The chick squawked in fright and scurried to Bea's side.

'That little saur is going to set this whole lot alight.' Theodore shuddered.

'It's just a chick,' Bea said.

'Trust me. This will become a feeding frenzy, and we're right in the middle. If attacked, every saur here could fight back. A steg can swipe its tail spikes; tritops and stytops have horns for protection. Even a phalox headbutt can break bones and hurt a tyrant. That thing may one day grow up to be the king of the savannah, but right now it's easy prey.'

A second, louder roar seemed to shake the ground beneath them. It was closer and even more menacing than the first. The Ronax quickly started to chat back to each other in lightly raised barks that sent a shiver of fear down Theodore's back.

The crowd of saurs became more restless. There was a bone-shaking roar, and from between the packed saurs stomped the largest White Titan Tyrant Theodore had ever seen. Every saur took a step backwards to make room as it raised its head for a deafening roar.

'It's the missing male.' Theodore's voice trembled a little.

Carter stepped forward.

The White Tyrant swung its head down, and right up to Carter, who calmly stepped over the chick, to face its fearsome father. The chick popped its head between Carter's knees and let out a little chirp. The tyrant breathed in deeply through its nose, filling its lungs, and then let out another roar.

As the tremendous sound died down, the stegosorcerer opened his eyes up and looked about.

'Good. Before I was worried I had it wrong. They have not come to eat you.' He waggled his long finger at Carter. 'They have come to greet you!'

Carter smiled. The White Tyrant rubbed its head up to the chick, held its enormous jaws wide open and coughed up a lump of partially digested food onto the floor, which the chick took a mouthful of.

'Okay, happy families, but now what?' asked Theodore.

He counted at least eight or nine tyrants, all in close proximity, and hundreds of saurs still wide-eyed and startled. The White Tyrant smelt something new and swung its head round. The Ronax broke out into a frenzied chatter of barks and the horned tyrant started to tut loudly.

A sinister, low chattering noise from the crowd was followed by the sight of the unmistakable dark shape of a Black Dwarf Tyrant, which ran up to and around the White Tyrant like an overexcited Jack Russell terrier, its dark red tongue hanging out from between its jaws.

Bea's face lit up. 'Buster!'

Carter jumped with joy as the tyrant, frantic with delight, ran around and around before rolling over in the dirt and onto its back. Carter bounded over and rolled about on top of it. All the Ronax Tyrants broke cover and pushed up to the front to see what the fuss was about, and stared. The Lonesome Horned Tyrant stopped tutting, but kept its mouth open. The White Titan Tyrant tilted its head and shook it with disbelief.

The stegosorcerer looked around and laughed out loud. 'Saurs in harmony!'

Theodore shook his head. 'Four types of tyrants and no fighting … impossible.'

'The impossible is possible,' said Bea wisely.

All the saurs had dipped their heads and were now silent. Even the tyrants were passive, except for Buster, who was panting like mad.

Suddenly an apatosaur craned his long neck down in front of the other saurs, ducked its head right into the middle of the open circle, and gave Carter a gentle nudge. Carter was panting from rolling about with Buster, but he caught his breath and reached out his hands, and ran them over the apatosaur's humped brow. It leant in and nudged Carter again. Carter lifted his leg and slung it over the back of its head. The apatosaur raised its head and lifted Carter high above the crowd of saurs, who all looked up at him. At that, they all started to call out. Honks, barks, chatters, roars and calls filled the air. The noise became deafening.

A second apatosaur nudged Bea in the back, sending her off balance. She steadied herself by grabbing onto it, and was scooped up as it, too, lifted its head up. Suddenly she was up in the air with her brother, and the extent of the spectacle was revealed to them both. From high above, the gathered mass stretched back thirty or forty saurs deep all around them. Carter whooped, tears of joy streaming down his face. Bea broke into laughter as they were turned around by the appatos, above all the saurs.

Theodore sidled up to the stegosorcerer, who was rubbing the dust from the stone set in his necklace, making it sparkle.

'The end is not the end, just as the beginning was not the beginning,' said the stegosorcerer. 'My visions have been clouded. There were holes I did not see.'

'Well, *my* hole caught a very bad man,' Theodore said.

'Good, then my hole was built to fail, so that your hole would succeed.'

'No. Your hole caught him first, then mine, but he still got away,' sighed Theodore unhappily.

'Maybe that is the purpose of holes?' the stegosorcerer said. 'Not to catch, to fail catching.'

'Why are your answers riddled with more questions?' Theodore asked him.

'This bad man, his path runs with yours. Find him again.'

'Oh, I'll find him, rest assured I will,' said Theodore grimly.

The stegosorcerer was silent, then he said quietly: 'I have not always been a Steggi. Long before, I was a Saurman.'

Theodore nodded and realised the odd-looking stone the stegosorcerer was fiddling with was an opalised dinosaur bone.

'The message I carry is not for the saurboy, but for you, Mr Logan.'

Theodore blinked. 'Me?'

The man nodded.

'Trust what it is that you fear to be true. Guide the boy. It is your destiny as well as his.'

'But I don't understand.'

'Find the truth about the keystone you carry, the same way I found you at the sacred temple tree.'

'Are you saying that *I* am a Saurman?'

The stegosorcerer rested a hand on Theodore's shoulder and looked deeply into his eyes, as the children laughed joyfully high above them.

'The boy carries too great a burden. You must both help him. Your paths are the same, and you have much to learn. The girl will help teach you to unlock the faith.'

'Bea?'

The stegosorcerer smiled.

'Someone has to look after you both, Mr Logan.' He laughed. 'You cannot do this as well.'

A feeling of relief swept over Theodore, and for the first time since the swarm and fire, he laughed out loud with his fellow Saurman.

And Ranjit, watching in astonishment, said to himself in wonder: 'The impossible is possible.'

35

The Sauria Aviation Corporation

~ fear in its eye ~

Lake Victoria

Christian Hayter inspected his cargo. The krynos spines had been carefully cleaned and packed into wooden crates.

'Bishop, where are the steg plates I stole from that fat fool?'

'They're hidden underneath the legit stuff, just in case some official decides to open a box.'

Hayter nodded. 'Good. Nail the lids down.'

The next large crate lined up on the dockside had a swarm of flies around it. It also stank. Hayter grimaced.

'I think it's starting to turn, boss,' said Bishop. 'Nothing I can do 'bout it.'

'It would've lasted if you'd bagged it up as I told you to,' grunted Hayter. 'The viscount wants his trophy.'

The last crate was the biggest.

'Make sure it has air to breathe – don't cover it up,' said Hayter, peering into one of the air slits on the side, and

— 310 —

checking the White Titan Tyrant chick was still sedated.

'What of the Ronax chick that followed me out of the cave?' Hayter enquired.

'It's already landed, boss; it went with the kruger blades, ahead of us, with the doctor,' Ash replied, as he and Bishop loaded the crates into the hold of the Sauria Aviation seaplane, packing them around the chick's crate.

Viscount von Lamprecht Knútr walked up the gangway.

'All set?' he asked.

Hayter nodded.

'Good. Is it still alive?'

Hayter nodded again, and helped the viscount into the front of the plane, before squeezing himself into the back. He looked at the pilot, who was studying the gauges, a concerned expression on his face.

'What's the problem?' Hayter asked.

'We're overweight. I could dump some fuel, but that'll mean we won't get there.'

'Ash. Bishop.' The Viscount beckoned them over.

'Yes, sir?'

'Can you fly?'

The two men loooked at one another, puzzled.

'Fly? Like, as if we had wings?' Bishop laughed. 'No, sir, of course not.'

'In that case, you'll have to swim. Hayter, throw them out, will you?'

Hayter grinned.

'As you wish, boss. Er ... Viscount.'

And he made for the two shocked men, his bullhook in his hand.

✦ ✦ ✦

Hundreds of glass eyes lifelessly watched the viscount from the mounted hunting trophies that lined the hall. A spark flew out from the glowing fireplace and he extinguished it under his polished shoe.

'Darling, I can see your hunting trip was successful!'

The Viscount turned to greet Anya, his pale, pristine wife, who wafted in and kissed the air around him. 'But is there room for any more in here?'

The viscount smiled.

'I was just thinking of extending the grand hall. I've spotted a few more specimens that have interested me greatly.'

Anya studied the latest addition, a mounted head, proudly placed above the fireplace.

'I do like this one,' she said. 'They have stuffed it very well. I can see the fear in its eye from the moment you shot it, darling.' She turned to her husband and adjusted his white bow tie. 'Forgive me, you know I'm bad with saur names. What is it again?'

The viscount looked up at the new head, and gave a proud smile.

'A White Titan Tyrant.'

✦ ✦ ✦

THE END

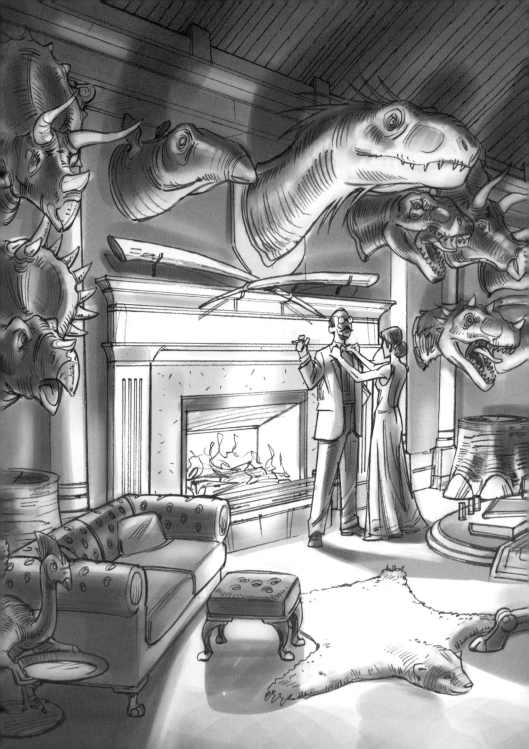

Excerpts from
Saurs of the Wild

~ *by Nigel Winsor* ~

ALLOSAUR
Carnivore | Biped

These theropod saurs, closely related to carnotors, have large but narrow heads on short necks, barrel chests, slender forelimbs with three claws, powerful hind legs (with three weight-bearing toes) and long tails. On their heads, distinctive ridges along the top of the nasal bones culminate in a pair of short, stubby horns above or in front of their eyes. These horns are covered in a keratin sheath and perform a variety of functions, including shade for the eye, display or combat against other members of the same species. The strong lower jaw is loosely articulated, permitting it to bow outwards and increase the animal's gape. With characteristically large nostrils and a keen sense of smell, these carnivores can smell rotting meat over a 50-mile distance. Thin, sharp teeth are perfectly designed for stripping a carcass. Allosaurs have neck and forearm feathers, and bony, feathered ridges along their neck, spine and tail. With the exception of a small group of Picayune Allosaurs, they have no ankle feathering, but lightly scaled skin with hardened scutes (hardened bony external plates) from the top of their toes to the knee.

Arabian Allosaur

Originating from the desert climate of the Arabian peninsula in south-west Asia, and prized by the nomadic Bedouin people, often being brought inside the family tent for shelter and protection from theft, the Arabian Allosaur is widely considered to be the purest breed of allosaur. The Arabian holds its head high on a long neck, with low brow horns. Its spine ridges are smaller and feathers softer than the European, with thinner forearm feathers and longer legs creating a streamlined shape. With its quick, sporting stride, Arabians are also the fastest breed of allosaur. Breeding Arabians have been used to improve other lines of allos by adding speed, refinement and endurance. Today, Arabian bloodlines are found in almost every modern breed of riding allosaur and they are one of the top ten most popular allosaur breeds throughout the world. Selective breeding for desirable traits, including its ability to form better cooperative relationships with humans, created the modern Arabian: good-natured, quick to learn and willing to please, with the high spirits and alertness needed in a saur used for raiding and war. This combination of willingness and sensitivity requires modern Arabian owners to handle their steeds with competence and respect. Arabians dominate the discipline of endurance riding, and compete today in many other sporting disciplines. When prepared for sport, blinkers and sound guards help to temper their skittish nature and prevent competitive aggression towards other allos. Lightweight saddles placed high on their shoulders help allosaur riders turn quickly.

European Allosaur

Characterised by thick spine ridges down its neck and tail, a thicker set of forearm feathers, short sprouts of feathering along its spine and very short brow horns, this easy-to-train, domesticated carnivorous saur has become as indispensible to mankind as the horse or dog. Fossil evidence suggests that early Europeans shared mutual hunting grounds with allosaurs, as bones have been found bearing both allosaur teeth marks and flint axe marks. Anthropologists believe it is likely both species adapted to sharing rather than competing for the same abundant food source. Folklore and myth suggest a strong belief in early Europeans that human spirits resided in allosaurs and thus were strictly off-limits as a food source. The European Allosaur gained confidence and became curious of humans, which eventually led to the mutual respect that is missing with other carnivorous theropod saurs like carnotors and tyrants.

The slim hips and girdle of the European Allosaur allow them to be ridden in a similar way to a horse. Commonly their spine feathers are plucked around the hips to allow saddles to fit with ease. The European Allosaur has been bred to become much less nervous and sensitive to sound than its Arabian cousin. However, early experiments with selective breeding also unwittingly caused undesirable traits to develop: loose jaws can become easily dislocated or misaligned, causing great discomfort when eating, and enlarged saliva glands mean most allosaurs dribble excessively.

1 Thinhorned Tritops
2 European Allosaur
3 Arabian Allosaur
4 African Red Stytops

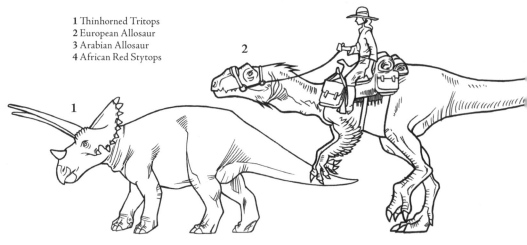

BRACHIO
Herbivore | Quadruped

Brachios are a distinctive group of sauropods, with disproportionately long necks, short tails, steeply inclined trunks and small heads with a large brow bump. Unlike most sauropods, brachios' forelimbs are longer than their hind limbs, resulting in their sloping body. They have five-toed forefeet with a single claw on the first toe, and three-toed hind feet with claws on each toe. Their robust, wide muzzles and thick jaws with spoon-shaped teeth allow them to strip foliage easily. Their long necks mean feeding on foliage well above the ground is preferred, but many are known to also strip away at low-lying shrubs when taller trees are scarce. Brachios carve long grooves in the ground with their feet and lay a line of eggs in communal nesting sites. The partially buried eggs are guarded by elderly females, which also take on the role of rearing the infants. Reducing the number of adults around the nesting sites helps to sustain enough vegetation for the remaining guardians to eat.

There are four types of brachios, identified by the landmass they originate from. The Indian Brachios is most common as it is

3

4

the smallest and simplest to train. The biggest of the brachios is the South American or Latin Brachio. Spanish conquistadors looted eggs as well as gold, and introduced them to Europe. This resulted in African and Indian brachios interbreeding. The only true pure-breed brachio left in the world is the Yucatan Brachio, a small population of which resides in the dense jungles that link Mexico, Guatemala and Belize. The African Brachio differs from the other types of brachios in three ways. They have a longer and thicker neck set into bulkier shoulders, and a higher brow bump. In appearance, the African Brachio looks remarkably like a cross between a giraffe and an elephant, and is the largest creature to dominate the continent. The large nasal cavity within its brow bump allows sound to resonate, and its cry can be heard over great distances. Surprisingly African Brachios are great swimmers and will swim miles around the coast to get to lush grazing sites, and can often be found cooling down in waterholes and enjoying mud baths.

CERATOP
Herbivore | Quadruped

Ceratops are split into three groups: hardtops, stytops and tritops. Their body shapes differ between the groups, but all ceratops have strong tails, bony frills that flare backwards over and around the neck, and short, strong limbs with three hooves on each forefoot, and four hooves on each hind foot. Tritops are the largest and most common, and have three horns, which vary in orientation between subspecies. Stytops have shorter horns than tritops, but are also horned on the bony frills of their necks. They are generally found in hot climates. Hardtops lack both brow and nose horns but usually have single or double frill horns.

African Red Stytops

African Red Stytops is the common name for all African stytops. It is hard for anyone visiting Africa today to imagine that once, not that long ago, all African stytops had no red skin markings at all. Gene sequencing tells us that at a relatively recent point in the Africans stytops' lineage, a new dominant 'red face' gene from the Asian Red Stytops was introduced. It is thought that, around 1840, a few Asian Red Stytops were introduced to North Africa by Egyptian traders. Within thirty years, red-faced stytops started appearing in central Africa, and by 1890 the population had spread to the southernmost point of Africa. The super gene has now virtually eliminated the species' original pigmentation. Northern African stytops tend to have a larger proportion of red covering the top half of their bodies. By contrast, the southern African stytop has much less red on its torso. It is therefore thought that as the 'red face' gene has spread, its dominance has been slightly diluted through interbreeding. Between regions, different subspecies of stytops can be identified by their boney frill horn variations, and are named in a variety of languages as every tribe or village farms using these docile and placid saurs.

Thinhorned Tritops

The Thinhorned Tritops (or Thinhorn) is the most agile of all tritops and significantly different from all other ceratops, as it has evolved to be quick-footed and agile to avoid predators in its natural habitat of sub-Saharan Africa. Its extremely long spiral brow horns (the thinnest and lightest of all horned ceratops) offer nothing in the way of protection, and its third nose horn is diminutive and unremarkable in comparison. Its bony frill protrudes further back than other tritops, and is flat at the sides to sit close to its slender frame. Most Thinhorned Tritops are dusty white to light tan in colour, with dark brown legs, with the exception of those that populate the regions around Lake Victoria. The majority of their time is spent on the water's edge feeding on the lush vegetation. A higher than normal consumption of aqueous bacteria and beta-carotene affects their skin pigmentation, turning these Thinhorns light pink like the flamingos that also populate the area.

PTEROSAUR
Omnivore | aerial

Lappet-faced Pterosaur
This scavenging pterosaur feeds mostly from animal carcasses. The Lappet-faced Pterosaur finds carcasses not by smell but by sight, observing vultures circling and then swooping in. They are the most powerful and aggressive of the African pterosaurs, and vultures will usually cede a carcass to the Lappet-faced Pterosaur if it decides to assert itself. Despite their advantage, Lappet-faced Pterosaurs frequently wait until the vultures are done, then feed on the remaining skin, tendons and coarse tissues that other scavengers will not eat. Lappet-faced Pterosaurs are often victims of persecution by humans and are often shot or poisoned by farmers who wrongfully fear they will kill their cattle or by poachers who fear the presence of these pterosaurs will alert authorities to their illegal activities.

Saddle-billed Pterosaur (Kongamato)
These large inland pterosaurs can be found living close to large lakes and waterways and are locally known throughout Africa as Kongamato ('breaker of boats'). Fishermen often have to fight off Kongamato that are taking the opportunity of an easy meal by swooping on the catch hauled into their boats. Their sharp pointed beaks often spear more than the fish, causing all sorts of damage. Saddle-billed Pterosaurs have bold black and white markings over their bodies, with bright red and yellow beaks.

STEGOSAUR
Herbivore | Quadruped

Stegosaurs are characterised by distinctive spikes and plates that cover their bodies. These saurs have small, long, flat narrow heads with a horn-covered beak supported by a low-slung neck adapted for eating grass and low fauna. Their front legs are shorter than their hind legs, which elevates the tail. Some species have a long shoulder spine in front, curving to the rear. Running down their necks, backs and tails are two rows of either offset or paired vertical keratinous-covered bony plates and spikes in a variety of sizes. At the rear of the tail, pairs of spikes form a formidable defensive weapon. Bony scutes cover most of their body and help protect soft tissue. Native to Africa, the group is most commonly represented by their largest example, the majestic stegs, who have formed a symbiotic relationship with humans and live side-by-side with nomadic African tribes. However, other smaller varieties of stegosaurs exist, and though the stegs are the most commonly recognised, in fact, the kruger and krynos are both members of the stegosaur family. In contrast to their larger cousins, both krugers and krynos are independent of humans and form large family groups in the wild known as crowds.

Krugers

Krugers are identified by long, thin or elongated diamond-shaped bony plates along the necks, backs and upper half of the tail. These pairs of 'blades' are placed at evenly spaced intervals. They also have hard scutes, shaped like stubby horns, along the body, forming an outer row to the blades. These scutes elongate at the bottom of the tail and form bony tail spines, which offer protection from predators. Krugers are predominantly found in southern Africa, but some Diamond-back Krugers will migrate north and can be found grazing on the pastures surrounding Mount Kenya.

Krynos

Krynos have a distinctive shoulder spine, or 'spike', which offers protection from large predators, but a less flexible tail and shorter tail spines than other stegosaurs. There are twelve types of krynos widely spread across Africa, each with subtle differences in their plate orientation and spike length, which is thought to be related to regional differences in landscape around the vast continent. The twelve regional varieties of krynos are further split into a somewhat confusing amount of different, and often repeated, Biblical names. For example, there are known to be 35 different types of Peter's Krynos, 32 types of James's Krynos and 28 types of John's Krynos. The origins of their naming after Christ's disciples is a mystery, as most tribes that keep krynos are not Christian. Differences between these subspecies are too small to be of note.

Stegs

The largest of all stegosaurs, and the most widely recognised, is the East African Steg, characterised by its large, wide tear-drop or kite-shaped bony plates, and its pale, dusty light grey to beige skin (often adorned with markings made by the tribespeople it lives with).

These plates line its neck and rise over its back, first increasing and then decreasing in size along its outstretched tail. Its tail ends with four long, bony outward-facing spikes, used only in defence, and they have no shoulder spikes.

What is remarkable about stegs is their symbiotic relationship with the Steggi, a large group of nomadic tribes found predominantly in Kenya and other central and eastern regions of Africa. Outside this relationship with the Steggi, there are no wild stegs – it is a totally unique co-dependency. In a form of dominant domestication, stegs no longer perform many parental duties that would have been natural to them. The Steggi remove all the eggs each steg lays, and select half to eat. These are claimed to be still eggs that won't hatch. Great care is bestowed on the remaining eggs in a hatchery, where they are cared for by the children of the tribe. From the hatchery, all eggs usually hatch and bear live young. The tribe then cares for them in infancy too, assuring them of reaching maturity. Adult stegs are cared for throughout their lives. If the Steggi tribes were to

1 Kryno
2 Kruger
3 Steg

leave this cohabiting relationship, they would certainly adapt and survive, albeit by living a different existence to the one they know. But the stegs would soon become extinct without their human companions, as vital reproductive and caring functions would cease to be conducted.

Many studies into this unique relationship between human and saur have all produced different findings. In 1908, Peter Williams, a famous British biologist, managed to persuade a small tribe of Steggi to conduct a test. A female steg was isolated from the herd and left to lay her own eggs and tend to them, which she did seemingly without distress. The steglets hatched, but only half survived the first day, and of the remaining half, only another fifty per cent lived to the end of first week. This female steg appeared to have no mothering skills. The Steggi tribe became so distressed after a week that the experiment was stopped and the remaining steglets were cared for by their human companions back in the tribe's hatchery. It is impossible, however, to say what percentage of steglets would survive in the wild, if they were not cared for by humans. As a comparison, for example, studies of wild krugers show that only half of their eggs hatch, as most get taken by predators, and a similar percentage of their young will die within the first week of hatching.

Human assistance in rearing and protecting stegs has the side effect that no natural predators exist for these large saurs. There is a widespread opinion in many African regions that the Steggi's way of life results in an overpopulation of stegs, and authorities have tried to enforce culls. This has met with much opposition, both from the Steggi tribes and groups around the world, who believe that the authorities behind the culls are influenced by financial considerations. No conclusive evidence exists as to a natural population level for stegs.

Nomadic herds of stegs often graze on the land used by cattle and stytop farmers. Stegs are protected by law, but to drive the Steggi away farmers often illegally shoot stray stegs on their land, citing self-defence from the risk of injury or death from the stegs' formidable tails. A dead steg can subsidise a farmer's livelihood as steg plates fetch huge sums of money on the black market; the money involved is more than most people earn in a year. Corruption at high levels mean many farmers, officials and politicians see an untapped profitable resource in dead stegs.

TYRANT (AFRICAN)
Carnivore | Biped

Lonesome Horned Tyrant

Suitably named, the Lonesome Horned Tyrant lives alone and is aggressive towards everything except a female in heat, and this urge to reproduce only arises once every eighteen months. Usually it warns off anything approaching with a menacing sound it creates with its tongue, much like a rattlesnake. Its impressive triangular brow horns widely protrude from the skin above its pale blue eyes, shielding them from the scorching African sun. Below its brow horns, this tyrant also has large pointed cheekbones, which it uses when attacking its prey – or anything that gets too close – with swipes from its huge head. The second largest of the tyrant family, the Lonesome Horned Tyrant is believed to be the oldest species. Mature adults are known to have lived for over 200 years. Currently their numbers are perilously low. Ever-shrinking habitats force these solitary creatures closer together and thus to their death, as most then kill each other. Efforts to increase their numbers in recent years have failed. Most safari parks and reserves can only accommodate one, and, unless carefully managed, breeding programmes are also prone to failure.

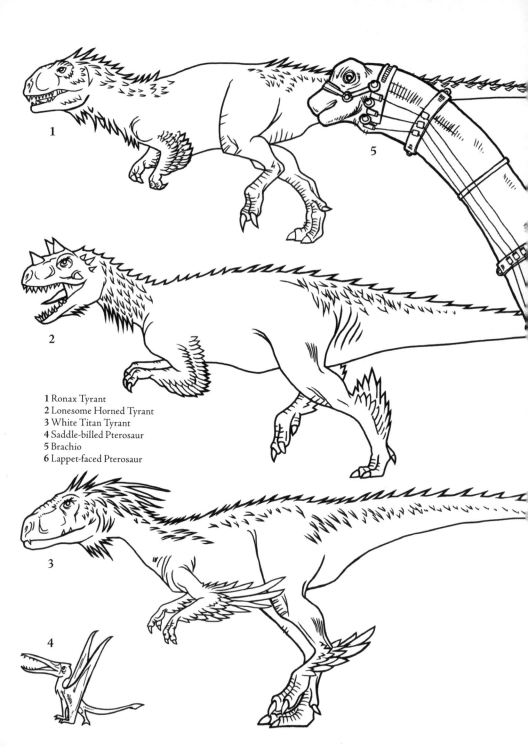

1 Ronax Tyrant
2 Lonesome Horned Tyrant
3 White Titan Tyrant
4 Saddle-billed Pterosaur
5 Brachio
6 Lappet-faced Pterosaur

However, unlike most horned animals and saurs, Eastern medicine has no use for their horns. The Lonesome Horned Tyrant's low sex drive means that, unlike other horned creatures, who are symbols of virility, it is not prized and so safe from illegal poaching. This is probably why this curious saur has not already become extinct.

Ronax Tyrant

Tyrants around the world are known for their solitude, isolation and reluctance to form social groups of any kind. More than one tyrant in close proximity leads to a territorial battle, and the tyrant who emerges dominant eliminates the opposition. Ronax, the smallest of the African tyrants, are the exception to this rule. Found only in the eastern regions of Africa, these carnivorous bipeds live in groups known as 'a rack'. Studies show that when isolated, Ronax quickly become distraught and harm themselves. Being part of a rack of extended family members works well for the Ronax. In the open

6

landscape of their natural habitat they benefit from having eyes in many locations, and hunt together to bring down their prey. Their rust-red, tan and brown mottled and striped body feathers help them blend into their surroundings. Males have blacker heads and feet than females, but in the dust of their natural environment this is very hard to spot. Naturally, as a consequence of living in groups, Ronax have the largest vocal range and most developed communication skills of all the tyrants, vital in organising hunts when camouflaged in the open bush. Ronax, assisted by their powerful neck and jaws, can often bring down prey many times their size through their unwillingness to let go once they have attacked. No creature is off-limits, even African Apatos or African elephants. The White Titan Tyrant may be known as the 'Emperor of Africa', but faced with a rack of Ronax it will soon walk away from confrontation. For these tyrants, travelling, hunting and living in a group has indisputable benefits.

White Titan Tyrant

Native to Central Africa, the White Titan Tyrant is one of the largest of the species, with mature adults measuring up to fifteen metres long. Its back is covered with matt white feathers, which help to reflect sunlight, and its underside is almost featherless, to help keep it cool. A White Titan has long, ridged ankle and forearm feathers, and elongated feathers on its elbow joints to allow it to prune and scratch the feathers down its back and tail that its head cannot reach. Females are smaller than males, and have no display feathers on their heads. Unusually for tyrants, the male White Titan will help to build and protect the large open nesting holes, clearing a large space around them so that predators will have nowhere to hide, and thus assuring its offspring gets the best start in life.

The White Titan Tyrant has become a global symbol of prestige and power, and is often referred to as the 'Emperor of Africa'. It is a ferocious and formidable wild saur, and has not been domesticated. History tells us that Roman emperors once rode them to demonstrate heroic bravery. However, the truth behind this great feat is not so impressive. Some adventurous Romans began to capture and breed White Titans, to satisfy the fashion for exotic creatures to be slaughtered in the gladiator pits. Through careful selective breeding, they attempted to draw out some of the White Titan Tyrant's aggression, so they would be easier to handle and kill in the barbaric games. But it was after the discovery of a cocktail of toxins, derived from snake venom, that it became possible to sedate the tyrants in a semi-conscious coma, rendering them docile and passive. The masses, unaware of the sedative, believed that only emperors were brave and able enough to ride White Titan Tyrants. Parading around before the games on a sedated White Titan Tyrant was a privilege afforded to Roman emperors for 160 years, until 193AD. Nine weeks after his predecessor, Pertinax, was assassinated, Emperor Didius Julianus was riding his White Titan Tyrant in front of adoring crowds. Word had spread that Didius Julianus had paid the Praetorian Guard to kill Pertinax. His enemies sought to ensure that the venom used to sedate the White Titan was diluted. The White Titan bucked, causing Didius Julianus to fall, whereupon his tyrant ate him in front of the horrified onlookers. Some historians have pointed to this event as a catalyst for the Fall of the Roman Empire. Whatever the truth, certainly no one was foolhardy enough to ride a White Titan Tyrant ever again.

✦ ✦ ✦

COMING SOON

THE WORLD OF
SUPERSAURS
CLASH OF THE TYRANTS

A Wild West adventure awaits . . .

L. Jóin

L. Kwa

Kampala Ft
Mengo
Ripon Falls
Ft Thurston
Port Alice
Port Victoria

R. Terminus
KIBIGORI
Ft Ternan
MA
Port
Florence
KIBOS
MUHORONI
LUMBWA
MOLO
EL BURGON
NJC
ELMENT

ENTEBBE
Steamer Route

Sesse
Ids

VICTORIA

NYANZA

Shirati
Mori R.

Budoba

Steamer Route

R. Mara

BRITISH
EAST
AFR

ANG

GERMAN

Ukerewe I.

R. Ruwana

Speke G.

Natron L.

Mwanza
R. Simiu

Smith
Sound

L. Eyasi

SCALE OF GEOGRAPHICAL MILES

0   20   40   60   80   100   120   140   160